JUDITH PERKINS

The Glass Ceiling Chronicles

Payne Construction

EXPLORA BOOKS
700 – 838 West Hastings St. Vancouver, BC V6C 0A6
www.explorabooks.com
Phone: (604) 330 6795

ISBN: 978-1-997587-06-4 (Paperback)
978-1-997587-07-1 (eBook)

JUDITH PERKINS
The
Glass Ceiling
Chronicles
Payne
Construction

Table of Contents

Cast Of Characters

Sylvia Payne	Owner of Payne Construction
Geraldine Rogers Payne	Mother of Sylvia – ex-wife of Thomas Payne
Thomas Payne	Father of Sylvia Payne – deceased
Jerome Browning	Attorney for Sylvia Payne
James Murray	Attorney for Geraldine Payne
Jason Gorman	General Foreman – Payne Construction
Roberta Robinson	Private Secretary for Sylvia Payne
Boyd McGregor	Judge – Multnomah County Court
Shirley Monroe	Sylvia's best friend
Justin Howard	Shirley's boy friend
Darren Polk	Geraldine's friend – on parole
Joe Crawford	Employee of Payne Construction
Linda Crawford	Joe's wife
Mrs. Johnson	Sylvia's Neighbor
Raymond Larson	Detective with Multnomah County Sheriff's Office

David Fallon	Insurance Adjuster for Vandalism claim
Michael Victor	Genoa-West restaurant owner
Mr. Storm (Stormy)	The Payne's Gardener
Jeff Range	Owner – Ranger Plumbing Services
Jon & James Powers	Powers Brothers Electric
George Chamberlin	Deceased Security Guard
John Stevens	Jason's friend and owner of Security Company
Bill Bowen	Arson Investigator with Multnomah County
Dr. David Martinson	Sylvia's Doctor
Luke Gregson	Geraldine's rich boyfriend

CHAPTER 1

It was February 14, 1970, Valentine's Day, and Sylvia Payne was all alone. She was in her office at Payne Construction, trying to figure out the papers that were in front of her. They were legal papers from an attorney hired by her mother, who apparently was trying to take control of Payne Construction away from her. Her mother thought that she was too young and incompetent to run the company.

Sylvia's father, Thomas Payne, had started Payne Construction when he was 22 years old and had built it into the mega-million- dollar company it was today. The company was based in Portland, Oregon, but worked jobs all over the Northwest. They built large strip malls and office buildings in the tri-state area and had up to 150 men working for him at a time.

Sylvia had been involved in the business since she was 16 years old and knew the ins and outs of running a construction business almost as well as her father did.

Geraldine Rogers Payne was Sylvia's mother and Frank Payne's ex-wife. They had been divorced for two years when Frank was killed in an auto accident a year ago.

Geraldine had given up any rights to the company when she divorced Frank in favor of a large monthly alimony payment. Upon Frank's death, the payments stopped. Frank was very generous in the divorce settlement, but complete ownership of Payne Construction went to Sylvia Payne, Frank's daughter, along with sole ownership of his home.

Sylvia had a college degree in Business Administration and a master's degree in marketing and was fully capable of running the business, but Geraldine thought she was too young and incompetent to run a successful business. Geraldine was asking for sole ownership of Payne Construction, cutting her daughter out completely.

Sylvia was aware it was Valentine's Day, but she steered away from romantic involvements now. She was too busy running the business, and it looked like she would be wrapped up in legal problems also. Her father had worked too long and hard for her to lose the business now.

All of a sudden, her office door swung open, and Geraldine stormed in.

"Get out of my office, Mother!" Sylvia demanded.

"Sorry, my dear. I have every right to be here. Probably more so than you. I have a paper here that states your father and I were in the process of reconciling at the time of his death. That makes me as much of an owner of this company as you are," Geraldine announced, waving a piece of paper in front of Sylvia's face.

Sylvia grabbed the paper from her mother's hand and read it. It was a handwritten note from Geraldine to Frank begging for a reconciliation and professing her love for him and their daughter, that all she wanted was to be a family again.

"I know you, Mother! All you want is money. Now that your alimony checks have stopped, you are getting desperate that you won't be able to continue with your extravagant lifestyle. Any money this company makes goes back into the company. I do not even take a salary. I am living off of the trust fund that Grandma and Grandpa set up for me," explained Sylvia. "Anyway, I do not believe this note. It is a handwritten note by you. You could have written it this morning for all I know. It doesn't help your cause any that you were off with one of your many boyfriends when Daddy died. Some reconciliation!" Sylvia pronounced.

"Well, you can't even get a boyfriend!" Geraldine huffed. "You are probably still a virgin."

"I am and proud of it," announced Sylvia. "I don't sleep around like you do. No wonder Daddy divorced you. He did not want to be married to a slut."

Geraldine reached over the desk and slapped Sylvia across the face. Sylvia snapped her head back, put the palm of her hand up to her stinging face, and said very softly, "Get out of my office!"

"It will soon be my office, and you will never set foot in it again," Geraldine muttered as she walked out of the office.

Growing up was difficult for Sylvia. She was introverted and could never seem to live up to the expectations of her outgoing mother. Geraldine had enrolled Sylvia in ballet and tap dancing lessons, had put her into gymnastics classes, and had tried to get her to participate in the social activities that the elite of Portland society took part in, but none of them had any appeal to Sylvia. She loved to read and took her studies in school very seriously. During her junior year in high school, she applied and was accepted to Stanford University in Palo Alto, California. Thomas was so proud of her for her accomplishments, but Geraldine was not happy that she wanted to go to college instead of advance in the social scene in Portland.

Sylvia graduated with honors from Stanford and went on to get her master's degree in marketing with the idea of joining her father's company and one day helping run it with him. Little did she know that she would be running it by herself so soon.

CHAPTER 2

Thomas Payne had spent all of his adult life building his business into the success it was today. He started the company when he was 22 years old, doing simple remodels and additions to homes in the area. He had tried college but could not afford to continue. His parents were not able to support his sisters and him, so they had to go to work. His mother was not well, and it was all his father could do to get her the medication that she needed. He worked as a janitor in the Portland Public Schools.

Thomas had shown some skills in carpentry work in high school shop class and decided to hire himself out to do small remodel jobs. He did good work, and his clients were pleased with the end results. They recommended him to others, and eventually, he had more work than he could handle by himself. He hired a friend to help, and as more and more referrals came his way, he had to hire more workers. Eventually, one of his clients suggested that he start a business and really make some money doing construction work. With the help of a customer who was an attorney, he formed Payne Construction, and off he went.

Thomas' business continued to grow. He met and married Geraldine Rogers three years later, and ten months after the wedding, Sylvia was born. Thomas was over the moon about his baby daughter, but Geraldine was less than enthusiastic about being a mother. She was still young and wanted to be out partying all of the time. Sylvia was left with a babysitter most evenings while Geraldine was out on the town, and

Thomas was busy working and trying to run his company. Many evenings, he would take Sylvia to the office with him to finish his work. He had a crib and changing table set up in an alcove of his office for her.

Eventually, Thomas and Geraldine separated. Sylvia rarely saw her mother. She spent most of her time with Thomas. There were several reconciliations between her parents throughout the years, but they were never a loving couple, especially around Sylvia.

Sylvia attended Cleveland High School in Southeast Portland, and during her junior year, she applied to Stanford University in Palo Alto, California. She received an acceptance letter in her senior year. Thomas was so proud of his daughter.

Thomas was a good golfer and enjoyed getting out on the course for a round of golf with friends. Many times, he would take Sylvia with him, and she learned to play a decent game of golf. Another activity that Thomas enjoyed was elk hunting. In October 1969, he was on an elk hunting trip with friends when he tripped over a log and fell down a cliff, breaking his neck as he fell. He was killed instantly.

Sylvia was devastated at the news of her father's death. Geraldine was nowhere to be found. After three days, they finally found her in Hawaii with a new boyfriend.

Geraldine appeared at Thomas' funeral all dressed in black, on the arm of her attorney, sobbing at the death of her beloved husband and announcing that she was ready to take over the reins of the company. Much to her surprise, when the will was read, she learned that Thomas had made a new will naming Sylvia sole heir to the Payne Construction Company. She also had sole ownership of the home that she was raised in.

Geraldine was livid. The business was everything that she wanted, and she was determined to get it, no matter what she had to do to her daughter to reach her goal. She swore that she would contest the will and gain control of the company.

Geraldine hired an attorney and proceeded to file a claim to contest the will, claiming that Sylvia was too young and incompetent to run a business as large and valuable as Payne Construction.

The company's attorney was sure that the will that Thomas had made before his death was ironclad and could not be contested. The note that Geraldine had given to Sylvia stating that she was reconciling with Thomas was not enough proof that she and Thomas were getting back together.

With Sylvia's master's degree in business and marketing, it was going to be hard to prove that she was incompetent to run the business.

Geraldine was keeping up a steady stream of negative publicity about Sylvia and Payne Construction, hoping that it would cause Sylvia enough anxiety to make errors in running the business. She could then capitalize on the mistakes made and attempt a takeover.

Sylvia was well aware of what her mother was doing. The negative publicity was a distraction, but she was able to keep on schedule with the construction jobs that she had and was able to successfully bid on a new strip mall being built in North Portland.

The employees that Sylvia had were extremely loyal to her. She had kept them all on the payroll since Thomas' death, and it looked like they would be able to continue to work. The North end of Portland was a depressed area, and this mall would provide needed resources for the community. Over 50% of the businesses in the mall were presold, and the remainder were under consideration when the construction started. A laundromat, a locksmith, a vintage clothing store, and an income tax preparer were among the shops already contracted to occupy offices in the mall. It was a good start on lifting the economy of the area.

Many of the employees that Sylvia employed lived in the area of the new mall, so the local workers made the project more desirable to the area. There was an article written in the Portland Oregonian newspaper about Sylvia and Payne Construction and the work they were doing in that area of Portland.

Geraldine was so angry when she read the article that she called the newspaper to give them a story about Sylvia that would refute the information in the article. She wanted to hurt Sylvia's reputation and that of Payne Construction so that she would have leverage to take over the company and right the possible wrongs done to her.

Unfortunately, the story that Geraldine gave the newspaper reporter was all a lie, and she was caught up in it. Geraldine had claimed that Sylvia did not have a valid master's degree from Stanford and that she was a fraud. She also claimed that the bid that Sylvia submitted for the strip mall construction was incorrect and that she would never be able to meet the requirements and keep within the budget allotted.

Sylvia was so angry when she read the story, but she tried to keep calm while phoning her attorney. "What can I do about this article?" Sylvia asked Jerome Browning, her attorney.

"We can absolutely refute the master's degree statement. You have a valid diploma from Stanford University, and the school can verify it if necessary. As far as the bid, a lot depends on who your mother is using as an expert on bidding for jobs and the experience they have. You have pulled experts from every facet of the business, and they are all very experienced in their fields. You have put together a very sustainable bid. If your mother is trying to undercut you, then she has to be figuring on using inferior building materials and cutting corners on some of the aspects of the construction. If you want to take this to court as a defamation of character lawsuit, we can get ahold of her bid information and check out the sources and materials she would be using. We could also check out the subcontractors she would be hiring," explained Jerome.

"I am so angry right now, I am willing to file a defamation lawsuit, but what would that do to the reputation of Payne Construction?" asked Sylvia.

"You might take a hit, but it wouldn't last long. Your quality of work and the company's reputation will hold up in any court of law," stated Jerome firmly.

"Ok! Let's go ahead and file a lawsuit against her. I am sick of all of the crap she is pouring on me. It is taking away my time from work. I need to concentrate on the jobs I have in progress now and on some that I would like to bid on," Sylvia said.

CHAPTER 3

Geraldine Payne was at her hairdresser's when a man walked in and asked the receptionist if Geraldine Payne was there. The receptionist pointed her out, and the man walked over to her. "Are you Geraldine Rogers Payne?" he asked.

Geraldine looked up from her magazine and said, "Yes, I am.

Who are you?"

"This is for you," the man said, handing her an envelope. He turned around and left the salon.

"What the hell?" Geraldine gasped with a surprised look on her face. She then opened the envelope and yelled some profanities, then sat back down to read the papers that were in the envelope. She muttered to herself, "That little bitch. She cannot do this to me. She has no grounds to sue me for defamation."

Geraldine snarled at her hairdresser, "Hurry up and finish what you are doing. I have to see my attorney immediately."

James Murray heard Geraldine storm into his reception area and yell at his secretary that she needed to see him immediately. Fortunately, he was not on the phone or busy with a client. He could tell something had happened, and he was pretty sure he knew what it was. Geraldine had a mind of her own and did not take advice very well. He had told her not to talk to the reporter, that she would be subject to a liability lawsuit, but she did not listen to him.

"Jim, look at this load of crap I was just handed. At my hairdresser's salon no less!" Geraldine spouted. "I have never been so embarrassed. That girl will regret doing this to me."

"Calm down, Geraldine," Jim told her calmly. "I told you not to talk to that reporter, but you would not listen to me. She has every right to sue you, and I would have been surprised if she had not."

"Well, she will regret going against me. I will take her down a peg or two. I will ruin that business if she persists in this stupid lawsuit. Everything I said to that reporter is true. Sylvia doesn't have a master's degree from Stanford. She never finished. She is lying about that. And she doesn't know how to bid a project. She will lose her shirt if she continues to underbid all of her competitors," Geraldine announced in a loud voice.

"Geraldine, Sylvia does have a valid master's degree from Stanford. She did finish all of her classes, and her grades were excellent. She was fourth in her class. She just did not participate in the graduation ceremony. Thomas had just died, and she needed to come home. You were not here, and she had to make all of the arrangements for his funeral and manage the business. And according to her bottom line, she is doing a good job of it," Jim explained.

"That's beside the point," Geraldine exclaimed. "That business should be mine, and I want it. She has no right to be running it."

"Geraldine, if you persist in this pursuit of ruining your own daughter, I want nothing to do with it. You cannot win this lawsuit. With verification from Stanford about the validity of her degree and looking at the financial figures for the business, you do not have a leg to stand on. Give it up! Enjoy the life you have now," Jim said.

"Jim, I need that business. I do not have an income now without the alimony checks from Thomas, and the inheritance is not going to last forever. I must have a steady income, and the business is the way I can have it. Please, help me get it," Geraldine purred as she sidled up to Jim.

"This won't do you any good, Geraldine. I told you not to talk to that reporter, but you didn't listen to me. I told you that your allegations were false, but you would not listen to me. A client who does not listen to or take her attorney's advice is a client I do not want to represent," Jim stated firmly.

Geraldine sat down in a chair and started to cry.

"Tears will do you no good!" Jim stated firmly. "You need to find a lawyer who is gullible enough to believe you. That attorney is not me."

"I cannot believe that she is competent to run that business. She is too young and inexperienced. The girl has no business working with men. For God's sake, she is still a virgin," Geraldine stated with venom in her voice.

"And what does being a virgin have to do with running a successful business?" Jim questioned.

"How can she deal with men without knowing about men?" asked Geraldine.

"Sylvia is running a successful business because she doesn't have her mind on sex all of the time. She keeps her concentration on the business and only that. She is a very intelligent and wise young lady and is a good businesswoman," stated Jim firmly.

"I am going to fight her any way I can. I want my name on that business. I deserve it for all of the crap I took from Thomas for all those years. He should not have changed his will. That business is mine," said Geraldine firmly.

"Well, you will do it without me. I will not help you ruin your daughter or her business. If you persist in this folly, I will not be your attorney any longer. You will have to find someone gullible enough to believe you," said Jim as he stood and walked to the door to escort her out of his office.

"Along with taking over Payne Construction, I will ruin you. You will not practice law in this town again after I am through with you," Geraldine yelled as she stormed out of Jim's office.

CHAPTER 4

Sylvia had given instructions to the construction superintendent and his job foremen that Geraldine was not to be permitted access to any of the job sites or any of the plans or specs for the construction that was currently in progress. She wanted to make sure that Geraldine could have nothing to twist around and use against her.

She also had a private meeting with each of the foremen to explain the situation. They all knew that their salaries and those of their workers were higher than most other construction companies in the area.

"My mother is trying to take over the company. She wants money, and the only way she thinks she can get it is by owning this company. I told you all at the time I took over running Payne Construction that I would not take a salary. All of the profit made on our jobs goes back into the company. Part of that is your salaries and those of the workers. I will always support the unions that you all are members of. I feel that it is important that you have that representation, and I will always negotiate in good faith with your union representatives. My mother does not support the unions, and she has said to me that I pay all of you way too much. If she gets control of this company, your pay will be lowered, and she will try to do away with the unions. I am afraid there will also be layoffs," Sylvia explained to each of them.

"Because of some of the things that my mother has said to the press, I am filing a lawsuit against her for personal liability and defamation of character. The company might take a hit because of it, but it will only be temporary. The publicity will not be favorable to us because of what she has said, but we will bounce back, and I assure you that all of your jobs are safe," Sylvia assured them.

"We are all behind you, Miss Payne. We appreciate the care and concern that you show us and like working for you. You treat all of us fairly," one of the foremen said.

"Thank you for your support. I wanted you to know what was going on in the company. Thanks for coming in today. This process might take a little while, but we will be okay and much stronger for the experience," Sylvia said as they all filed out of the conference room.

Sylvia went back to her office to work on a proposal she was preparing for a new off-site Emergency Room affiliated with Providence Hospital in Portland. The specifications were different than your normal office building. There would be smaller examination rooms, central nurses' stations, and an x-ray lab. Sylvia had done quite a lot of research on emergency rooms and knew what she had to do to successfully bid on this project.

She called Jason Gorman, her construction superintendent. He had worked for her father and was at the top of her list of trusted employees. Jason would know how to successfully bid on this project. He had helped build the small hospital in Cedar Hills, just southwest of Portland.

"Jason, how's it going? This is Sylvia. Are you available tomorrow to give me some advice? I need your expertise on a bid I am putting together," asked Sylvia.

"Sure! I can be there at 9:00 A.M.," Jason answered. "Looking forward to seeing you then. Thanks," replied Sylvia.

Sylvia continued to work on the bid, figuring the amount of lumber needed, the nails, screws, nuts, and bolts, and all of the accessories that would be needed to complete the framework of the building. She was working on developing a list of subcontractors when her phone rang.

"Roberta, I asked not to be disturbed. What's up?" asked Sylvia. "Your mother!" Roberta exclaimed. "She's on her way up to your office."

Just at that moment, Sylvia's office door slammed into the wall when Geraldine opened it with force.

"You bitch!" Geraldine yelled. "You had me served with your stupid papers in the middle of my hair appointment. You embarrassed me to the core. I will ruin you for this."

"Will you please come in here, Roberta, with your notepad and make a record of everything my mother and I say to each other, including what you just heard over the intercom?" asked Sylvia very politely.

"I will be right in," Roberta answered quickly. When she walked into Sylvia's office, she gently closed the door and went to sit down in the chair beside Sylvia's desk.

"Thank you, Roberta," Sylvia said very quietly and politely.

Geraldine was standing there, getting red in the face; she was so angry. She was also put off guard by Sylvia's demeanor. She had thought that her forceful actions while entering the office would rile Sylvia up and cause her to say or do something that she could use against her daughter. Obviously, her hysterics did not work on Sylvia.

"Now, Mother, what was it that you wanted to talk to me about?" Sylvia asked in a very polite tone.

"You embarrassed me when you had that process server come to the salon to give me those papers. I did not appreciate that at all, and you will regret doing that. I am going to ruin you and this business, Sylvia. You are incompetent to run the business, and all of the blame for the downfall of Payne Construction will go to you. You are a fraud," yelled Geraldine.

"I am sorry you feel that way, Mother. The process server went to your home but only found your current boyfriend there. I remembered that you have a standing appointment at your salon for the same day and time every week. I told him to try there to find you. By the way, he said that your boyfriend answered the door only in his boxers. You might warn him that some of your other boyfriends might stop by. It would not be good if he was found there in that state of undress," Sylvia warned.

"You bitch!" Geraldine murmured as she stormed out of the office. Roberta heard some papers go to the floor as she looked at Sylvia in amazement.

When Roberta saw her desk, she saw several files scattered on the floor. Geraldine must have swept them off as she walked by.

"I knew your mother had a hot temper, but I have never seen it in action before. That was quite a show!" Roberta exclaimed. "I cannot fathom a mother treating her daughter the way she does."

"She has done that all my life. Not quite as extreme as this, but she put me down every chance she could get. I know she resented me from the time I was born. Mainly because Daddy was so happy. He really doted on me, but without spoiling me too much. I went everywhere with him before I started school, then I was with him after school and on weekends. Mother would take off to some exotic place, angry that Daddy would not go with her. She said they could hire someone to take care of me while they went and had a good time. He was building the business and had to be here to take care of it. He also said that he was not going to have some stranger raising his daughter," Sylvia explained. "So, Mother went off on her exotic vacations, sometimes for a month or two, and Daddy took care of me and his business."

CHAPTER 5

Roberta typed up the notes from the conversation that Sylvia had with her mother. The secretary for the foremen was a notary public, so Roberta decided to be on the safe side; she would have her signature on the form notarized. If this mess ever went to court, it might be needed as evidence against Geraldine. She could not understand why a mother would do this to her own daughter. Where was the motherly love? She apparently had none.

After the notes from the conversation with Geraldine were finished, Roberta took them into Sylvia. "Here is a copy of the notes from the conversation with your mother. I had my signature notarized just in case the notes would be needed in court."

Sylvia was sitting with her back to the door, looking out the window at the Portland skyline. She marveled that some of the smaller buildings in the city were built by Payne Construction while her dad was still alive and running the company. She remembered going to the job sites with him. Sylvia slowly turned her chair around to acknowledge Roberta. "Thank you, Roberta. I hate to put you in the middle of this mess, but I thought I had better have a witness to that encounter. I am so angry at this situation and at her that I might have slugged her." Both Sylvia and Roberta laughed at that statement.

"I almost did!" stated Roberta.

"Thanks for thinking about having the statement notarized. I hope this does not go to court, but if it does, it is liable to get nasty and cause some negative publicity for the company. Jerome Browning says we might take a hit, but our reputation is sound enough that it should not last long," Sylvia explained.

Roberta left Sylvia's office thinking about Geraldine and her accusations against Sylvia. She just could not understand how a mother could act that way towards her own child.

Sylvia got back to the bid she was working on for the off-site emergency room. She was trying to put together a figure for the materials and was having a hard time concentrating. Her mother had caused her to lose her train of thought, and she had to get it back. She still had the labor portion of the bid to work on, and she had to factor in all of the subcontractors she would need.

The hospital's specs showed eight exam rooms. Each room had to have a sink, so there would have to be proper plumbing for each of the rooms, plus the normal bathroom and breakroom plumbing. She would have to choose a top-notch plumbing contractor for this job. The same would be needed for the electrical part of the bid. The electric specifications were complicated for an emergency room, and again she would have to hire an electrician who was top of the line.

After figuring the materials part of the bid, Sylvia had to work on the labor part. That was sometimes more complicated than the materials. She had to figure the amount of time needed to complete each phase of the job. She would have to consult with the subcontractors she chose to do the job. It was all very confusing, but she was a well-organized person and knew the process needed to get the bid in on time. This particular project would be a good one for Payne Construction to build an even bigger and better reputation than they already had. She just hoped that this mess with her mother did not put a stop to the process.

Just as she was thinking about completing the bid process, her intercom rang. Roberta announced that Jerome Browning was here to see her.

"Show him in, Roberta," Sylvia announced.

"Hello, Jerry. You look grim this afternoon," Sylvia said sarcastically.

"Your mother takes the cake. She has filed a countersuit claiming you defamed her character and caused her mental harm by having the process server give her those papers at her hair salon. I think public humiliation was mentioned in there somewhere also," Jerry explained, giving Sylvia a hint of the reason he was paying her this visit.

"I know you are busy getting the Providence bid ready for submission, but these papers are important. They need to be answered as soon as possible."

Sylvia stacked the papers on her desk in a neat manner and put them in her center drawer. She was very careful about the confidentiality of her calculations, even from her attorney.

"Okay! I am ready." She sighed as she pulled up her chair and sat down to look at the papers he handed her.

"These need to be dealt with in a timely manner. I really do not want to rile this lady any more than possible. She really is a force to be reckoned with. She is demanding three million dollars for the damage she says you have caused to her reputation. If we pay her the three million, she will drop all of the charges," Jerry said.

"Three million? Where does she think I am going to get three million dollars? The business is doing well, but not well enough to take three million out of it for her to spend on her vacations and her lovers," Sylvia said with venom in her voice. "I will go to court before I give her three million of this company's hard- earned dollars."

CHAPTER 6

The court date that was set for the preliminary hearing on the lawsuit brought by Sylvia Payne and Payne Construction against Geraldine Rogers Payne was set for May 12, 1970. Sylvia was frustrated because she had not heard anything about the bid she submitted for the new Providence off-site Emergency Room. There were four companies presenting bids, and Payne Construction was the only local company bidding. One was from Seattle, and the other two were from California.

Geraldine had made sure that there was a lot of publicity regarding the upcoming trial, and it was not favorable to Payne Construction, its founder, or its current president. There were constant newspaper articles spreading rumors and lies about her ex-husband and her daughter, even stating that there was something improper between father and daughter.

"I cannot believe what she is saying to the press. She is manufacturing lie after lie about Daddy and about me," Sylvia complained to her attorney. "She thinks something is wrong with me because I have never had a steady boyfriend. She has had enough to satisfy twenty women. I am really sick of her telling me there is something abnormal about me," complained Sylvia.

"Please do not worry now. We will refute all of it in court. She will not be able to prove any of the accusations she has leveled against you," Jerry reassured her.

Sylvia was at the office all weekend doing some last-minute checks on projects that were just about finished. She was proud of the work they had done on a strip mall in Oregon City. It was a beautiful building and was 85% occupied already, with only two offices left to rent. Sylvia was happy with the final result and how it looked.

Roberta was working with her that weekend. Both of them wanted to get some of the backlog finished so they would have the time free for the trial. Roberta was going to be an important witness during the trial. She had taken notes and had them notarized every time Geraldine stormed into Sylvia's office with some wild idea or complaint. She was ready to present all of these pages of notes as evidence that Geraldine was not telling the truth and was unstable herself.

Sylvia left the office about 3:30 PM on the Sunday before the trial was to start. She wanted to try to be well-rested before she went into court. She had inherited her father's home near Reed College in Southeast Portland. She had lived in the house all of her life, and it was filled with all of her favorite things. Her house was near a golf course. Her father had taught her to golf when she was a teenager, and she loved the sport. She used to go with him almost every weekend during the good weather. She and one of her girlfriends still tried to get together to play at least once a month.

Sylvia's golfing friend, Shirley Monroe, was also single but had a steady boyfriend. She was always trying to match Sylvia up with one of his friends.

"Shirl, I am just not interested in dating now. I have too much on my plate with running the business and trying to deal with this lawsuit my mother has filed against me and the company," Sylvia explained the reason why she would not go out with Justin's friend.

"You need a distraction and to have some fun. You are working all of the time. It is not good for you!" Shirley complained. "You need to unwind."

"I am doing fine. I just need to concentrate on work and getting this thing with Mother over with," Sylvia explained to her friend.

"Oh well, maybe next time!" Shirley stated.

"See you soon, Shirl," Sylvia said. "I have a lot of work to do to get ready for the trial and don't know when I will be available for a golf game, but I will call."

Just as Sylvia hung up the phone, her doorbell rang. She went to the door, and as was her usual habit, she looked through the peephole. She saw her mother standing there with a man beside her. She opted not to open the door to her and to remain quiet so her mother would know that she wasn't home.

"Try the door, Darren. I want to get into the house. Hopefully, Sylvia will not be there, and I can look around and find some evidence against her. I need all of the dirt I can get to take her down," Geraldine continued prattling to Darren.

Darren tried the doorknob to see if it was unlocked. It was not. He pulled out a tool that he tried to use on the door lock, but he was having a hard time trying to get it open.

In the meantime, Sylvia had called the police to report a possible break-in. She asked them to turn off the sirens as they got closer to the house so her mother would not run away.

The police arrived just as Geraldine was pounding on the door, frustrated because she could not gain entrance.

"What are you doing here?" the officer asked Geraldine and Darren.

"This is my daughter's house, and I have not heard from her for some time. I am worried about her. She is not well and might be in trouble. I was trying to get in to check on her," Geraldine explained to the officer in a panicked voice.

"Are you Geraldine Rogers Payne?" the officer asked.

"Yes, I am. Please force the door open. I am terribly worried about my daughter," Geraldine replied.

"There is no need for you to worry, Mrs. Payne. Your daughter called just a bit ago to let us know you and this gentleman were trying to break into her home. You and your companion are under arrest for attempting to illegally enter a private residence that does not belong to you," the officer replied to Geraldine as he put her arms behind her back and put handcuffs on her. Darren was also put into handcuffs.

The police officer rang the doorbell, and Sylvia opened the door. "Are you okay, Miss Payne?" the officer asked.

"Yes, I am fine. Thank you," answered Sylvia.

"Oh Sylvia," cried Geraldine. "I was so worried about you. Please tell the officer to take these handcuffs off of me. I was not trying to break into your home. I was only worried about your welfare. You know you have a hard time taking care of yourself during stressful situations. I was only trying to help."

Sylvia ignored her mother completely and thanked the officer again, then closed the door.

She could hear her mother outside, screaming that it was all a mistake and she should not be taken to jail.

CHAPTER 7

Geraldine Payne did not have to spend the night in jail, but her companion did. He was arrested on parole violation for attempted illegal entry to a private residence. Geraldine claimed she didn't know that he was on parole and didn't know that he was going to break into Sylvia's home.

Sylvia did not believe her but let it go. She had enough to stress about with the upcoming court appearance and her increasing workload. Construction jobs were still being posted for bid, and she was trying for Payne Construction's share of the jobs. As she finished projects and the crews were released from their jobs, she wanted to have another project ready for them to step into. Sometimes it took a juggling act, but so far, she had been able to keep all of her employees working.

Jason Gorman was very good about helping her keep everyone employed. Most of her workers were married with families. Both she and Jason were very committed to keeping families together and healthy.

Jason walked into Sylvia's office one day with news that one of their employees had been hurt on the job and was taken to the hospital. "He was climbing a ladder to get to the roof of the building when he slipped and fell onto a pile of lumber. The paramedics said he has a concussion and a gash in the back of his head. He was conscious when they took him in."

"What hospital?" Sylvia asked as she arose, grabbed her purse, and started walking out the door.

"Emanuel's trauma center," said Jason. "I will drive you." "Okay, let's go!" Sylvia announced.

Sylvia and Jason arrived at the hospital to find Joe Crawford still in x-ray. He apparently hurt his shoulder as well as sustained a concussion.

Jason took hold of Sylvia's arm and led her to the waiting area. "Let's sit and wait until the doctor comes out." Joe's wife, Linda, was in advanced stages of pregnancy and was sitting in the corner of the waiting room in tears.

"Linda, I am Sylvia Payne. Have you heard how Joe is?"

"Not yet. The doctor said he would come out when he had read the x-rays. Miss Payne, I am scared. I am due to deliver any time now, and I need to have Joe with me. If he is hurt badly, I don't know what I will do. The doctor says he doesn't want me to drive until after the baby comes, and I depend on Joe to get me to the doctor and the grocery store. I am so worried that he will not be able to be with me when the baby is born," Linda cried.

"Let's wait and see what the doctor says. Jason and I will stay here with you. You will not be alone," reassured Sylvia.

Sylvia called Roberta and let her know that she was going to wait for word from the doctor about how Joe was. Roberta assured her that everything was okay in the office and she was not to worry.

"Roberta, I am afraid that my mother will hear about this accident and descend on the office to take over. Please have one of the security men at the front door to keep her out. Would you also go into my office and lock my desk? I do not want her anywhere near my office or desk," Sylvia asked.

"Of course. I will take care of it. Let me know how Joe is. He is a sweet boy, and with Linda about ready to deliver, it must be stressful for him," reassured Roberta.

Sylvia, Jason, and Linda waited for another thirty minutes for the doctor to come and let them know what was going on with Joe. When he did arrive, Joe was in a wheelchair right behind him.

"Joe will be fine. He has a slight concussion, but nothing that would warrant keeping him in the hospital. His shoulder has a deep bruise on it, but nothing is broken or dislocated. He needs to do some motion exercises every hour to keep the shoulder from stiffening up, but other than that, he should be fine," the doctor announced. He turned to Joe and said, "Remember, no work for the rest of this week. You will need to rest. Looking at your lovely wife, you will need to get your strength and energy back very soon anyway."

Linda was smiling, with tears in her eyes, and said, "Thank you so much, Doctor. I was pretty scared."

The doctor patted her on the arm and said, "He will be fine.

Good to meet you all."

Jason left to get the car and bring it to the emergency room door. He and Sylvia drove them home and then went back to the office. Sylvia called the finance office at the hospital and asked that the bill for any deductible that Joe would have to pay be sent to her, and she would pay it. She did not want Joe or Linda to worry about any extra expenses at this time.

Jason Gorman was 32 years old, tall with light brown hair. He was well-built and strong because of the work he did on construction sites. He had a good working knowledge of all forms of construction, carpentry, plumbing, electrical, roofing, and finishing work. That was why Thomas Payne had made him the foreman at such a young age. Shortly before Thomas died, he had promoted him to the company's Construction Superintendent.

Thomas had found him to be scrupulously honest and loyal as well. Jason was devastated when Thomas was killed. He stepped up and helped Sylvia with the transition of ownership, and Sylvia would always be grateful to him for that.

"Come into the office for a few minutes, will you, Jason?" asked Sylvia. "I want to talk to you about the court appearances coming up next week."

"Sure," Jason answered.

They both walked into Sylvia's office. Sylvia sat at her desk, and Jason sat in the chair on the opposite side of the desk.

"What's up?" Jason asked.

"It's this blasted lawsuit coming up next week. Would you be able to come to court with me?" asked Sylvia. "I hate to ask, but I need the moral support. It is so hard to sit there and listen to my mother spout all of the lies she is telling about me. They are not true, but I seem to have no words to defend myself. I would like someone there that is on my side."

"Sure, I will be there. I have some very reliable job foremen, and they can take over while I am gone. Do you want me to pick you up here? I will be happy to be on your side. I always have been," said Jason.

"Thanks," Sylvia murmured.

CHAPTER 8

Sylvia and Jason walked into the Multnomah County Courthouse together on Monday morning. Sylvia was grateful that Jason agreed to come with her. She was very nervous about confronting her mother in court. Geraldine had been saying some very nasty things about her, and some of them were very personal. She was not looking forward to answering questions from her mother's attorney.

Sylvia sat down at the table with Jerome Browning and saw that her mother was seated opposite her with her attorney and three other people. They were all conferring very quietly together.

"What are our chances of finishing this trial up today?" Sylvia asked Jerry.

"Very slim. Geraldine has a long list of witnesses she wants to have testify against you, going back to your high school days. She says that they will testify to your lack of morals, to an inappropriate relationship with your father, and to the fact that you have a fake degree from Stanford University," explained Jerry.

"Good God! She is fabricating everything. I can't believe that she would think that Daddy and I had any kind of relationship except that of father and daughter. That is so far-fetched, it is ridiculous," Sylvia cried.

The courtroom was called to order by the bailiff, and the judge walked in. He asked if all the parties involved were in the courtroom. After hearing affirmative answers on both sides, Jerry was asked to proceed for the prosecution's side. Jerry called Roberta, who presented as evidence of Geraldine's slander and defamation of character the notarized notes that she had taken during the outbursts that Geraldine had made in Sylvia's office. Jason testified as a witness to a couple of Geraldine's outbursts at construction sites. Then Sylvia was called to the stand.

"Miss Payne, will you tell us about your relationship with your mother when you were a child?" asked Jerry.

"I did not really have much of a relationship. She was gone much of the time, and I wouldn't see her for weeks," Sylvia told the court. "Who took care of you?" Jerry asked.

"My father. Before I started school, I would go to the office with him. It is said that when I was a baby, he would carry me in a sling at his chest. After I was in school, I would be at the office with him before and after school. He would take me to school and pick me up afterward. He was just starting the business and could not afford a babysitter or a nanny," Sylvia explained.

"Where was your mother during this time?" Jerry asked. "Sometimes in Mexico, or Hawaii, or on one of the Caribbean Islands. She was always off on some holiday," Sylvia said as she looked over at her mother.

"You were the sole heir to your father's estate, including his company, Payne Construction, were you not?" Jerry asked.

"Yes. I had been working at my father's office since I was sixteen years old and knew the business inside and out. I had watched my father build the business into the success it is today. He left me 100% ownership in Payne Construction in his will," Sylvia explained.

"Was your mother to receive any part of the business?" asked Jerry. "No, she was not!" stated Sylvia firmly.

"Your Honor, I present a copy of the Last Will and Testament of Thomas Payne as evidence of Sylvia Payne's true and honest statement," said Jerry, handing a copy of the will to the bailiff to give to the judge.

"This looks like a certified copy of the Last Will and Testament of Thomas Payne," said Judge McGregor. "It also states in the will that Sylvia Payne is the sole heir of Thomas Payne and receives sole ownership of Payne Construction Company. I do not understand why this is a factor in this lawsuit," the judge questioned.

"Your Honor, Geraldine Payne is contending that she should own the company, as she was reconciling with the deceased at the time of his death, and that fact should make his will null and void," stated Jerry.

"I would like to question Mrs. Payne," said Judge McGregor. "Mrs. Payne, please take a seat up here."

Geraldine looked at her attorney with a question in her eyes. He motioned her to the witness stand. She had no choice but to go up there, although she had not prepared for this turn of events. She did not want to answer the judge's questions without knowing what the questions were and being able to prepare for them.

Geraldine sat down in the witness chair and gave a puppy dog look to the judge.

"Mrs. Payne, did you leave your infant daughter with your husband while you went on vacation?" the judge asked Geraldine.

"Well, yes, but if he would have just hired a nanny or even a babysitter, he would not have had to care for her, but he was too cheap to do that. I had to have a break from all of the work," Geraldine answered.

"How long were you gone, Mrs. Payne?" the judge asked.

"I was just gone for a month," answered Geraldine, displaying some amazement that the judge would ask a question like that. "It was not very long, and she seemed to be well taken care of. Anyway, babies that age only need to be fed and have their diapers changed. They don't know one person from the other."

"Mrs. Payne, why do you contend that your daughter does not have a master's degree from Stanford University?" asked the judge.

Geraldine answered, "Because she did not participate in the graduation ceremony. You have to do that and get your diploma before you have your degree. Anyone knows that."

"Are you a college graduate, Mrs. Payne?" asked the judge. "No, but I never had the opportunity to attend college," answered Geraldine.

"Why do you feel you are more qualified to run Payne Construction than your daughter?" Judge McGregor asked.

Geraldine looked at Judge McGregor with an astounded look and said, "Well, I am older and more experienced than she is. In the construction business, you are dealing mostly with men, and I know a lot more about men than my daughter does. She cannot keep a boyfriend and has never slept with a man. What could she know about men?"

Sylvia was mortified at what her mother had said. She blushed and put her head down on her arms.

The judge pounded his gavel and firmly said, "That is enough! I do not need to hear any more garbage from your mouth, Mrs. Payne. You have slandered your daughter in open court. You have lied about her to the press, and therefore, I order you to pay your daughter the sum of $500,000.00 as compensation for such libel."

"What I said was the truth!" screamed Geraldine. "I don't have that kind of money. She is the one with all of the money."

"Your Honor, may I speak?" asked Sylvia. "Yes, you may," answered Judge McGregor.

"I do not want any money from my mother. All I want is a public apology for the things she has said about me and for her to leave me alone. I do not want her to come into my office, nor do I want her at any of my construction sites," Sylvia asked sincerely.

"All right, I will rescind the order of payment and change my ruling to an order for Geraldine Rogers Payne to make a public apology for all slanderous statements made against Sylvia Payne. Also, I will sign a cease and desist order against Geraldine Rogers Payne from entering the office of Payne Construction or setting foot on any of the Payne Construction sites. Do you understand these orders, Mrs. Payne?" asked Judge McGregor.

"Are you saying that I can never visit my daughter at her office?" asked Geraldine.

"That is exactly what I am saying. You are not to set foot in her office building or on any of her construction sites," the judge reiterated.

"I understand," Geraldine said meekly.

CHAPTER 9

When Sylvia and Jason left the courthouse, there was a group of reporters waiting outside ready for a statement from Sylvia regarding the outcome of the trial.

Sylvia's only comment was, "No comment."

When Geraldine came out with her attorney, she smiled and posed for the reporters and cameras. When asked by one reporter from the Oregonian newspaper about whether she would apologize or not, she said, "I will not apologize for anything I said on the witness stand. Everything I said was the truth. No one, not even the judge, can make me say it wasn't. I do appreciate all of you listening to me. At least you know you are printing the truth."

Geraldine's attorney grabbed her arm and tried to pull her away toward the waiting car, but she resisted. "These nice people have been waiting to talk to me, and I will not disappoint them. I have something to say to them."

"Do you remember what you told the judge?" asked the attorney.

"I certainly did. I said that I understood, and that was all. I did not say that I would apologize for what I said. Everything was the truth. My daughter has no idea how to work with men and should not be running a business with mostly men working there," spouted Geraldine.

At that moment, a policewoman came toward Geraldine and said, "You are under arrest, Mrs. Payne, for contempt of court and ignoring the judge's orders."

"This is a joke, right? You have no reason to arrest me," Geraldine laughed as the officer was placing her in handcuffs. The news cameras were working overtime with their filming.

Once the handcuffs were on and Geraldine could not move her arms, she was becoming convinced that she was being arrested and started screaming at the police officer. "Get these off of me! My wrists and arms are hurting. Get them off!" she screamed.

Geraldine was escorted back up the courthouse stairs and into the building. Her attorney followed and just hoped that bail would be set so that his client did not have to spend a night in jail.

Jason and Sylvia did not see or hear the commotion. They had left in Jason's car to go back to the office. Sylvia was going to get into her car and take the rest of the day off. She did want to talk to Roberta for a few minutes and give her some instructions as to phone calls from reporters.

When she got to the office, Roberta handed her at least a dozen messages. "There goes my afternoon off. I suppose I had best answer these," Sylvia said as she waved the messages in the air.

The top message on the pile was from Geraldine. Jason walked into her office behind her and closed the door. "Why in the world would Geraldine be calling me now? She just had the pleasure of humiliating me in open court. Why would I call her back?" Sylvia said as she sat down in her chair and started to cry.

Jason walked over to her, lifted her out of her chair, and gave her a hug. Sylvia clung to him. She sobbed into his shoulder. "I am getting your shirt all wet," she cried.

"Don't worry about it. I'm not!" Jason said. He held her for a few more minutes, kissed her on the forehead, and sat her back down in her chair.

"Thanks, Jason. I am sorry for breaking down. I try very hard not to do that. The last time I cried in front of anyone was when Daddy died. I am embarrassed that I did cry."

"Honey, you cannot be stoic all of the time. You have a right to show your emotions sometimes. God knows that the comments that your mother said were enough to put anyone under. Are you going to call her back?"

"I don't know. Maybe I should," Sylvia answered.

Just then, the intercom buzzed. When Sylvia answered it, Roberta informed her that her mother was on the line and sounded absolutely frantic.

Sylvia picked up the phone and said, "Yes, Mother, what do you want? I am busy and don't have a lot of time to chit-chat with you."

"You have to come down to the jail. They have arrested me for contempt of court. I was just stating the truth, but the judge didn't agree. I need you to come and bail me out now. I cannot stay in this jail," Geraldine begged.

"Why in the world would you think that I would bail you out of jail?" asked Sylvia.

"Because I am your mother. You are supposed to. It is your duty as my daughter," Geraldine said.

"Well, this daughter does not feel duty-bound. Sorry!" Sylvia stated and hung up the phone. She turned to Jason and said, "Do you believe that? She was arrested for contempt of court, and she wants me to bail her out of jail."

"Don't think about her now. She will have to learn to take care of herself. Maybe she has a boyfriend who will post bail for her," Jason said.

"She probably has several of them," laughed Sylvia. "Let's concentrate on work for a change."

CHAPTER 10

Jason Gorman was a tall, blonde-haired, single man. He was 32 years old. He worked hard and believed in Payne Construction. He also believed in Sylvia as the president of the company. He felt a little funny about working for a woman, but he wanted to work with Sylvia. She was smart and very knowledgeable about the construction business, and so far, he was impressed with the jobs that she had gotten for the company. They were all good jobs and would keep the crews employed for some time.

Jason had had several girlfriends in the past, but had never had a serious one. His longest relationship had been seven months, and he was the one who broke it off. He had met no one who was even near his idea of someone he could spend his life with until he got to know Sylvia. She was different. She was intelligent and compassionate about her employees' welfare. Joe Crawford's accident was a case in point. Sylvia visited him several times and made sure that he and his family had all that they needed.

Family was very important to Sylvia. All the while she was growing up, she craved a close family like her friends had. Her father was the only stable member of her family. Her mother was never around, and when she was, she pretty much ignored Sylvia. So, when Sylvia took over the company after her father's death, her employees and their families were all important to her. She made sure that they had the time they needed to tend to their families' needs without hindering the time schedules of their construction jobs. All of her employees loved her for her kindness to their families, and they were extremely loyal to her.

After the debacle with her mother, Payne Construction lost two jobs that they had bid on. Jason knew it was because of the bad publicity that Geraldine had spread all over the newspapers. He felt so sorry for Sylvia, but there was not much that he could do. The bids that Sylvia submitted were good, fair bids, but the owners chose other companies to do the work, even though their bids were higher than Payne's bids.

Jason was trying to think of ways to cheer Sylvia up after the failed jobs. He finally came up with the idea of the employees writing a testimonial about the working conditions at Payne Construction and the security of their jobs because of Sylvia's commitment to them and their families. He asked the employees and some of the subcontractors to write letters about their experiences with Payne Construction and Sylvia Payne.

The response to Jason's request was overwhelming. Everyone he asked wrote a glowing letter to the Oregonian about the company and Sylvia's commitment to them and to their families' welfare. The newspaper wrote a Sunday feature story about the company and its policies, quoting passages from many of the letters sent to them. The newspaper's emphasis was on a successful male-dominated company being run by a young single woman. It remained to be seen what the public response would be, but the newspaper did a good job of talking up the good parts of Payne Construction.

Jason walked into Sylvia's office on a Monday morning with a big smile on his face. "Did you see the article in the Sunday paper?" he asked.

"No. I was here all weekend trying to figure out what I did wrong on those two bids we lost," Sylvia answered.

Jason put the paper on her desk with the article on the top. Sylvia looked at it and then looked up at him with a questioning look on her face. "Who wrote this?" she asked.

"Your employees wrote the letters. They believe in Payne Construction and in you as their leader. They wanted you to know that, and this was their way of trying to put out some of the fires that have been burning since your mother's debacle," Jason said.

Sylvia had tears running down her cheeks after she read the entire article. "Honey, please don't cry. This is a good thing," Jason begged as he put his arms around her and she laid her head against his chest.

Jason lifted her head up and looked into her tear-stained face. "You are so beautiful," he whispered to her and bent down to give her a kiss on the lips.

Sylvia pulled back, startled at the kiss. She looked into his eyes for a moment, then she kissed him back.

"I have wanted to do that for a long time," Jason murmured. "Me too! I just didn't know how to approach it. I am glad you took the initiative," Sylvia laughed.

"Now what do we do?" Jason asked. "You are my boss. How do we have a relationship around that?"

"We do our work the same as we always have. Here at the office and when I am at a job site with you, we are strictly professional. After hours can be a whole different situation if that is what you want," explained Sylvia. "We just need to be discreet considering all of the publicity that my mother has caused."

Both Jason and Sylvia sat down on opposite sides of the desk. They did have work to do and needed to concentrate on it, but it was hard considering the passionate kiss they had just exchanged.

CHAPTER 11

Because Sylvia would not post bail for her mother, Geraldine had to spend the night in the city jail. It was not a pleasant place to be. She quickly learned that her yelling and crying got her nowhere with the guards. They gave her a small pillow and a blanket, and she had to sleep on a hard bench along with four other women in the same cell. She was escorted to the ladies' room when she needed it and was incensed when she discovered there were no doors on the stalls.

At 9:00 AM the next morning, Geraldine was escorted into the courtroom for a preliminary hearing. "I am sorry, Your Honor, for my actions yesterday. I was very angry with my daughter and wanted to hurt her and the business," she stated to the judge. Her attorney had told her what to say and also told her not to deviate from it at all. The judge accepted her apology and released her on her own recognizance. Her attorney would be advised as to when she would have to be in court for the trial.

Geraldine turned to her attorney and said, "What trial? I thought this was the end of this whole mess."

"There will be a bench trial on the contempt of court charge, Geraldine. You still have to appear before a judge on that charge," Mr. Murray told her.

Geraldine's attorney, James Murray, led her out of   the   courthouse and to the parking garage where he had his car. She was spouting obscenities about her daughter the whole time they were walking.

James couldn't wait until this whole mess was over. He did not like Geraldine Payne, but because he was low man on the totem pole at the law firm where he worked, he was assigned the case.

James dropped Geraldine off at her home. She went in and immediately called Payne Construction to talk to Sylvia. Roberta informed Geraldine that Sylvia was in a meeting and would not be taking any of her calls. Geraldine screamed into the phone and slammed the receiver down.

"I will just go down there and give her a piece of my mind. She cannot treat me this way!" Geraldine said to herself. She took a shower and changed her clothes, throwing away everything she wore except her jewelry. The guards had taken that away from her to be put into a safe for the night. It was returned to her this morning before she went into the courtroom.

As far as Geraldine was concerned, this whole business was a big error. The police and the courts were making a huge mistake. She was not going to tolerate being treated this way. She would say what the judge wanted her to, but she didn't have to adhere to it.

Sylvia suspected some repercussions from her mother's antics. She was almost 100% sure that she would hear something from her, but she didn't think it would be so soon. Geraldine stormed into the front door of the office. As soon as Roberta saw her getting out of her car, she went to the front door to try to block her from entering the building, but Geraldine just pushed her way in.

When Sylvia heard her mother come in, she called the police and reported her non-compliance with a court order to keep away from Payne Construction offices or job sites.

"You are a sorry excuse for a daughter," Geraldine yelled. "You made me stay in that filthy jail cell all night. You would not even post bail for me. What kind of daughter treats her mother like that?"

"The police are on the way, Mother. Enjoy another night in jail. You are defying a court order right now," said Sylvia.

Just then, two police officers walked into the outer offices of Payne Construction.

"Geraldine Payne, you are under arrest for disobeying a court-mandated order to stay out of Payne Construction offices and/or Payne Construction sites," the officer informed Geraldine.

"You cannot do this to me. I will not spend another minute in that filthy jail cell," yelled Geraldine.

"If you are not quiet, you might be spending more than one night in that cell or one just like it," the police officer informed her.

As the officer escorted Geraldine to the patrol car, Sylvia walked back into her office and closed the door behind her. She had a ton of work piled up on her desk, but she needed some downtime. She knew that Jason was busy, so she called Shirley. Shirley was always game for a shopping trip, and that is exactly what Sylvia needed right now.

"Hi, Shirl!" Sylvia greeted her friend on the phone. "Do you have anything pressing on your schedule for today?"

"No, not really. I have some papers to read for work, but I can put that off. What's up?" Shirley asked her friend with concern in her voice. She was well aware of what Sylvia was going through with her mother.

"Another round with my mother is what's up. I need to do some serious shopping to get my mind off of all of this garbage. Are you up for it?" Sylvia asked.

"You bet! Anytime," answered Shirley. "Want me to pick you up?"

"That would be great. Pick me up here at the office, sooner than later if you can," Sylvia said.

"See you in 30 minutes," answered Shirley.

Sylvia hung up the phone and buzzed Roberta to come into the office. "I am going to take the rest of the day off. I need some time to unwind from all of this nonsense. Shirley and I are going shopping, and I am going to spend some money on myself for a change. I probably shouldn't, but I feel like splurging. Shirley will be here in about 30 minutes. I will straighten up some of these files on my desk, but most of it will wait. There are two files here that I need the bid forms typed up. Will you do it for me and screen the rest of my calls for me?"

"You go and have a good time with Shirley. Buy yourself something really extravagant and have some fun for a change. You have been working too hard and have had too much stress lately. You need to relax," Roberta told her.

"If Jason calls, please just tell him I am out with Shirley for the rest of the day. I don't want him to worry about me," asked Sylvia.

"Okay!" grinned Roberta. "I will reassure him that you are okay."

CHAPTER 12

Sylvia and Shirley had a great afternoon at the Lloyd Center Mall. All of the summer clothes were out and both ladies had fun shopping for clothes and all of the necessary accessories.

Sylvia didn't say anything to Shirley about her blooming relationship with Jason Gorman. She didn't want to jinx anything by mentioning it. She knew that Shirley had a hard time keeping a secret and would want to spread the news around to all of their friends. Sylvia wanted it to be private for a while until she knew where they were headed.

Shirley suggested dinner out, but Sylvia was bone tired after a day of shopping. She needed an evening of rest before she tackled all of the work on her desk tomorrow morning.

"Thanks Shirl. It was good to get away from the office and all of the fiasco with my mother. She probably is spending another night in jail unless she can convince one of her many boyfriends to bail her out. I certainly won't!" Sylvia emphasized.

"Good for you," Shirley answered. "You get a good night's rest. Enjoy all of your purchases, although I don't know what you will do with that little black dress you bought. You never go anywhere that requires a sexy little dress like that. You are a real stick-in-the-mud!" Shirley said as she giggled at Sylvia.

Sylvia went into her house, turned off the alarm system and locked the door behind her. She turned around and found her living room totally ransacked. Lamps were on the floor, broken, chairs were overturned. Her TV was shattered and all of her treasured knick-knacks were broken up all over the floor.

"What in the hell?" Sylvia cried as she hurriedly unlocked the door and went outside again. She wasn't sure whether someone was still inside the house or not.

She ran to the neighbor's house, pounded on the door, and asked to use the phone. "My house has been broken into and it is a mess. I have to call the police." Sylvia cried.

"Come in," Mrs. Johnson, Sylvia's closest neighbor said.

Sylvia called the police and it wasn't five minutes before she heard the sirens coming up the street. She went outside to show the policeman where to go. He directed her to stay inside while he did a search of her house.

After a few minutes, the officer came outside and over to Sylvia who was standing on Mrs. Johnson's front porch. "It looks like they ransacked your whole house. It is a real mess. I will need to have you go into the house and do a cursory review and let me know if anything valuable was taken. Most everything is damaged, even the kitchen appliances.

Sylvia asked if she could call her company superintendent to go through with her. She wanted Jason there.

"Jason," Sylvia sobbed. "Please come to my house. Someone broke into the house and did considerable damage. I need you here."

"Hold on sweetheart. I will be right there. Have you called the police?" Jason asked.

"They are here now and asked that I go in and let them know if anything valuable was taken," she sobbed. "Please hurry!"

"I will be right there," Jason said.

Jason arrived at Sylvia's house within ten minutes. He took her in his arms and tried to comfort her as much as possible.

"Why is all of this happening to me, Jason?" Sylvia asked through her tears. I have tried to be good to everyone and not cause anyone any distress, except my mother and I don't think she could have done this. As far as I know, she is back in jail. She came to my office this morning, and caused a disturbance. I called the police and they arrested her again for defying a no contact order."

"Don't count her out," the policeman said. She could have hired someone to do this. It looks like it was done by a professional.

If you had the alarm system on, they had to by-pass it someway and only a professional would know how to do that, unless your mother knew it and gave it to someone."

"I had the system installed after my Father died and I moved back here from school. She did not have access to the code and I picked a number that she would never guess," explained Sylvia.

"Please, neither one of you, do not touch anything. The detectives and fingerprint guys will be here soon and they will go over the entire house. Miss Payne, do you have someplace you can stay tonight?" asked the policeman.

"Yes. I can stay at the office. May I take some of my clothes and personal items?" Sylvia asked.

"Sure," Sylvia was told.

She went first to the safe in the den. Her father had kept all of his important papers in the safe and also some extra cash. There was also some valuable jewelry that belonged to Sylvia's grandmother that Geraldine did not know about. There was a specific book in the den that was the key to the safe that was behind a hidden wall. Her father had wanted to make sure that Geraldine did not find it.

Sylvia went to the book, moved it a certain way and a door opened to reveal the safe. It had not been opened and when she did, everything was still there. Whoever had broken in did not find it.

"I would suggest that you put your car in the garage and have Mr. Gorman here take you to your office," the policeman suggested. Jason handed him one of his business cards and Sylvia let the officer know that Jason had her permission to speak to the detectives for her.

Just as Jason was putting an overnight bag into the back of his car for Sylvia, the detectives showed up along with the forensic team. They were all introduced to Sylvia and Jason. The detective made an appointment with Sylvia for the next morning to take a statement from her and to get as much information as possible.

As Jason and Sylvia were leaving, Sylvia noticed a strange car parked three houses down on the opposite corner. The driver was sitting in the car, but was looking at another house across the street. She thought that was a little strange, so she got out a piece of paper and wrote down the license plate number and the make and model of the car. She would call the detective and let him know what she had seen.

CHAPTER 13

I am not taking you to the office. I am taking you to my house. I have a spare bedroom, and you can stay there. I do not want you to be alone tonight, Jason told Sylvia as he drove away from her house.

"Okay, but I have to call the detective right away. I saw a strange car parked at the end of the street, and I want to give the detective the license number," said Sylvia.

"Let's circle around and go back to the house right now and tell him. It would be better if he knew right away," Jason said as he turned the corner and went back to Sylvia's house. He pulled up to the front of the house and told her to wait in the car. He would go in and ask the detective to come out to the car.

Detective Ray Larson came out to see what information Sylvia had. "I saw this car parked at the end of the street just as we were leaving a few minutes ago. I have never seen it before, and it is unusual for strange cars to be parked on the street. I know most everyone who parks their cars on the street. There was someone sitting in the car, but I could not tell if it was a man or a woman. I did write down the make, model, and license number though," Sylvia said as she handed Detective Larson the piece of paper.

"Thanks. I will check it out. You need to get away from here if someone is watching your house. I will talk to you tomorrow," the detective said.

Jason pulled away from the curb and headed towards his house, but Sylvia said she would feel more comfortable staying at a motel for the night.

"Just for tonight, Sylvia. You are upset and nervous, and I want to know you are safe. Tomorrow you can check into a motel. Please, stay at my place tonight," Jason begged.

"Okay, I will for tonight. But please, let's not publicize the fact that I stayed at your house. I am afraid my mother would get ahold of the information and all hell would break loose," Sylvia conceded.

She noticed that the car was no longer parked at the end of the street when they drove by again, so maybe it was a false alarm.

Jason owned a house in Milwaukie, Oregon, just south of Portland in Clackamas County. It was a small house with two bedrooms, but very clean and tidy for a bachelor's home. And the yard was beautifully landscaped. You could tell that Jason took great pride in his home.

"Come in. I will put your bag in the spare bedroom. Have you had anything to eat?" Jason asked.

"No. I was shopping with Shirley all afternoon, but we decided not to stay out for dinner. I was tired and wanted to get home. Darn! I left all of my packages in the house. I dropped them at the front entrance when I saw the condition of the house," explained Sylvia. "After all the mess with my mother, I needed some downtime, and shopping with Shirley was fun."

"How about if I order a pizza?" asked Jason.

"Okay, but I am not very hungry right now. I am just very upset and frustrated and angry. Very angry. What have I done to deserve this? I couldn't see that anything was taken from the house. It was only vandalized. Why would someone do that?" Sylvia asked as she started to cry again.

Jason sat her down on the sofa and held her in his arms while she cried. Her space had been violated and all of her beautiful things had been damaged. A lot of the mementos that were damaged were her father's. She had grown up with all of those things around her. Now she would not have them anymore. As soon as the police were through, she would go in and try to salvage what she could, but most of her things were damaged beyond repair. At least they had not seen the safe, and everything in there was okay.

Sylvia did eat a couple of slices of pizza when it arrived. She didn't realize that she was hungry. Jason offered her a beer, but she opted for water to drink. She wanted to have a clear head.

In the morning, Jason found Sylvia asleep on the sofa. She had apparently gotten up in the middle of the night, wrapped herself in a blanket, and went out to sit on the sofa.

He went to the kitchen to start the coffee, then headed for his bathroom to get ready for the day. Sylvia awoke to the smell of coffee brewing and headed for the kitchen. She could hear Jason's shower running. She found a coffee mug in the cupboard and poured herself a cup, then went back out to the sofa.

She got a pad of paper out of her purse and started a list of what she had to do that morning. The first thing on her list was to call her insurance company. Then she had to let Roberta know that she would be late for work. She wanted to go by her house and get her car. She was not sure if the detective would let her into her house yet, but she wanted to try.

Jason came out of his bedroom dressed for his workday. "Good morning! I see you slept on the sofa last night. It was probably not the most comfortable place to sleep."

"I was too restless to stay in bed. At some point in the middle of the night, I must have fallen asleep. I woke to the smell of this marvelous coffee. Thanks," Sylvia said.

"You can use the bathroom if you want to, and I will fix us some scrambled eggs for breakfast," Jason said.

"Please don't go to any trouble for me. I usually don't eat much of anything in the morning. Coffee is fine," Sylvia assured him.

"You need your strength. You have a long, stressful day ahead of you," Jason told her.

Sylvia went into the bathroom to shower and get ready for her day. It was strange getting ready in someone else's home, especially Jason's home.

Sylvia ate her scrambled eggs and had to admit that they tasted very good. She had another cup of coffee and settled down at the table with Jason's telephone to her ear while she made her phone calls. Roberta was horrified at what had happened and let Sylvia know that she would take care of everything at the office.

After talking to Roberta, Sylvia called her insurance company and reported the break-in and vandalism. Her agent informed her that an adjuster would get in touch with her as soon as possible and would also connect the police detective assigned to the case. The adjuster would have to walk through the house with Sylvia to determine if anything was missing. Sylvia had never had to deal with homeowners insurance before. She had the same company that her father had, and he always dealt with them. She paid the bill every year, and that was the extent of her contact with them.

As soon as she was finished with her phone calls, she asked Jason to take her to the house so she could get her car. She had to make some arrangements for someplace to stay until her house was cleaned up and she could stay there. When she told Jason what she had planned, he said that she should just stay at his place.

"I don't feel comfortable staying with you, Jason. I want to keep our relationship quiet for a while longer. I do not want my mother to find out we are seeing each other. She could use it against both of us in some way, and I do not want to deal with any more of her slanderous comments right now. I have enough on my plate," Sylvia tried to explain to him.

"I do understand your position. I don't like it, but I understand. I want to shout it to the rooftops that I love you. I want everyone to know, but I will respect your wishes," Jason conceded.

CHAPTER 14

Sylvia was stunned that Jason said he loved her. He had never given her any indication how he felt. She had secretly been in love with Jason since he first started working for her father, but of course, she would never have acted on it.

There was a police officer on duty at Sylvia's house when she and Jason stopped to get her car. She showed the officer her identification and told him that she needed to get her car out of the garage so that she could get to work. The officer called Detective Larson to see if it was okay. He gave his permission, but she was not to go into the house yet. The insurance adjuster had contacted him, and they were going to make time that afternoon to inspect the house with her. Forensics had finished processing the house last evening, but the adjuster did not want anything disturbed until he toured the property.

"Thank you for bringing me over here to get my car. I appreciate it. I hope you understand my reasons for not staying in your home with you," Sylvia said to Jason. "I just want to keep whatever this is between us, quiet for a while."

While they were standing in the garage, Jason took her in his arms and gave her a loving kiss. "I understand," he said. "I love you, Sylvia, and I want to shout it from the rooftops, but I do understand."

"I love you too!" answered Sylvia. "Now, as your boss, get to work!" she laughed.

Sylvia got into her car and realized that the purchases she made yesterday with Shirley were in the car. She thought she took them into the house, but apparently not.

Before Sylvia went to the office, she stopped at a fairly decent motel close to the office and checked in. She couldn't tell them how long she would be staying, but they did not seem to mind. Her room was on the second floor of the motel, which made her feel better. She felt safer than she would have if she had been on the first floor. Then she stopped at a drug store to pick up a few necessities and went on to work.

As she walked in the door of the office, Roberta ran to her and gave her a big hug. "Are you okay?" she asked.

"I am fine, just a little rattled and very angry. My house is a mess. It will take some time to get it back to livable condition. Furniture was broken, upholstery was slashed, glassware was smashed, and Dad's mementos were broken into a million pieces. I am really sick about those. Everything else can be replaced, but some of those cannot," Sylvia explained.

"I cannot imagine who could be that vindictive," Roberta said. "How many millions of messages do I have to answer?" Sylvia asked.

"It's not too bad. They are all on your desk. You do have a 3:00 PM appointment with the insurance adjuster and Detective Raymond Larson to go through your house," Roberta explained.

Sylvia nodded her head as she walked into her office and closed the door. She picked up the phone and called Jason at one of the construction sites.

"I have a 3:00 appointment to go to the house with the adjuster and the detective this afternoon. Would you go with me? I am not sure that I feel comfortable absorbing all of that information by myself," asked Sylvia.

"I will meet you there at 3:00 sharp. Love you!" added Jason.

Sylvia grinned as she hung up the phone. She wasn't sure how long they would be able to keep their relationship quiet. It seemed pretty obvious how they felt about each other.

Jason met Sylvia at her house along with the insurance adjuster, David Fallon, and Detective Larson. They went into the house, and Sylvia was shocked all over again. Mr. Fallon went through and cataloged all the items that were damaged and/or completely destroyed. Sylvia looked around to see what was salvageable. There were a few items that she picked up that were still in one piece, but nothing of her father's.

"Detective Larson, were you able to track down that license number I gave you?"

"Unfortunately, the license plate was stolen. The number did not match the car it was on. The car make and model and the license number are on the watch list for all of the patrolmen, so hopefully we will hear something, but I am not hopeful. They have probably already switched the plate with another stolen plate," Detective Larson explained. "We will keep an officer posted 24/7 on this place for a while. I'm not sure if whoever did this was just creating havoc or had a specific purpose for the vandalism."

"It is beyond me why someone would do this. I can't figure out what I would have done to cause someone to commit such a terrible attack. As far as I know, nothing was taken. Thank goodness the safe was not found because all of the really valuable items were in it," Sylvia said.

Detective Larson was putting furniture upright as they toured each room. Occasionally, Mr. Fallon would ask Sylvia a question about a specific item, but most of the time, he was busy making his list.

When he felt that he had cataloged everything that was damaged, the three of them sat down at the upright kitchen table and discussed the process of settling the claim.

"The staff in my office is very good at finding comparable items, both in description and in value to use in settling a claim like this. Fortunately, you made sure that your coverage was updated. You have a $1,000.00 deductible, so you will have to satisfy that before a claim is settled. Did you just recently increase the value of the dwelling and personal property?" asked the adjuster.

"I have done nothing about increasing any value on anything. My father died almost a year ago. He must have increased the value before he died," Sylvia mused.

"No, the coverage was increased six months ago," David explained.

"Who called to increase it? I certainly did not. Insurance was the last thing on my mind six months ago," explained Sylvia.

"The file shows that Mrs. Geraldine Payne made the call and asked for the increase in value of both the dwelling and the personal property," said David.

"Do not pay her anything!!!" emphasized Sylvia to David. "That is my mother, and she has no claim on this property at all. When she and my father were divorced, she gave up all rights to the house and property, as well as the business."

Sylvia turned to Jason and asked, "Do you think that she could have done this?"

"She probably would not have done it herself, but she could have hired someone to destroy your home. She certainly has been vindictive enough. I bet just the fact that you would not pay her bail caused her to go ballistic," Jason said.

"Tell me what you are talking about," Detective Larson asked.

Sylvia proceeded to tell the detective and the adjuster what had happened with Geraldine within the last couple of weeks. "I am not sure where she is right now. She was in jail again for violating the protective order the last I heard. She did not have the money to bail herself out and had to wait for a hearing with the judge."

"Would she know anyone who would or could possibly cause this kind of destruction?" David Fallon asked.

"She could, I suppose. She does not have the kind of money she would have to pay someone to do this in broad daylight. The whole reason she is causing all of this trouble is to get money out of me and the business. I suppose she could have promised someone something valuable from the house, but there was nothing visible that was that valuable. Those things were locked up in the safe," Sylvia explained.

"Did your mother know about the safe?" asked Detective Larson.

"She probably knew that there was one somewhere in the house, but Daddy had the safe put in after they were divorced, so I am sure she didn't know where it was," Sylvia said.

"Well, my next job is to canvas the neighborhood and talk to your neighbors. Do you know of any of your neighbors who would be adverse to talking to me?" the detective asked.

"No. I have known them all my life. I have never lived in another house, and most of the neighbors have been here for a long time and knew my father well," explained Sylvia.

"Okay, I think we are done here. I would suggest that you not stay here until you can get a company in to clean things up for you. It will be too painful for you. We will have an officer watching your home for a while. I don't anticipate any problems, but we want to be on the safe side, and we want to catch the pervert who did this," Ray Larson said.

Sylvia and Jason thanked both the detective and the insurance adjuster as they left the house.

CHAPTER 15

Sylvia walked into the Payne Construction office knowing that her desk was going to be covered with messages. She met Roberta at the door to her office. Roberta looked white with fear when Sylvia looked at her face.

"What in the world is wrong, Roberta?" Sylvia asked with concern. "Your office was vandalized while I was out to lunch," Roberta told Sylvia in a very quiet voice. "I have not touched a thing. I am so sorry, Sylvia. As far as I can tell, nothing has been taken, but I am not sure what you had in your desk."

Sylvia turned pale and almost fainted when she heard the news. "I need to call Detective Larson," she mumbled. "Roberta, would you please call Jason and ask him to come to the office? Please do not tell him what has happened, just that I need him here."

She walked into her office and found a mess of papers all over the floor, some damage done to her desk and chairs, and all of the pictures torn off of the walls and smashed. They were all pictures that her father had before he died. Again, it seemed that the severe damage was done to the things her father had when he was head of the business.

Twenty minutes later, Jason came into the office. He asked Roberta what was wrong, but she just pointed him to Sylvia's office.

"Oh my God! This too," Jason said, exasperated at this turn of events. He was hoping that the office would be a safe place for Sylvia to work.

"I have called Ray Larson. He is on his way here. Again, the forensics will go over everything. Just glancing at things and not moving anything, I do not find anything missing. Just my papers strewn all over the floor and all of Daddy's paintings smashed to bits. You know, we did not keep any checks or cash in the office. Maybe that was what they were looking for, but they did not touch Roberta's desk or anything in the rest of the office. I am beginning to think that someone had a vendetta against Daddy," Sylvia commented.

"Your mother sure did," Jason said under his breath.

"I heard you, and yes, I agree with you. She certainly did have it in for him. His will was very explicit about the settlement of his estate. She was not to receive anything from the business, and that all payments to her stopped upon his death. He had the codicil to his will written just after the divorce was final. And he told her what he was going to do, so she was not caught unawares," Sylvia explained. "At this point, after all she has put me through, I would not put it past her to do something like this to the office and to the house."

"Sweetheart, I really do not want you staying at a motel by yourself. I don't think it is safe. Please come and stay at my place. It will be hard, but I promise to keep my hands off of you," Jason grinned at her. Right at that point, Detective Larson came into the office followed by Roberta.

"You were hit again, it seems," the detective said as he looked around the room.

"Yes. Most of the damage seems to be to my father's paintings. All of the damaged paintings were ones he had hung here before he died. Some of them were quite valuable. They could have been sold for quite a lot of money, but whoever did this opted to destroy them instead," Sylvia explained.

"The insurance adjuster, David Fallon, will be here shortly. I called him as soon as I heard from you. I am assuming he will want to marry the two claims as I am assuming they were caused by the same person or persons," Detective Larson said.

"I need to get all of these papers sorted out. I probably had ten different files on my desk, and all of the papers are jumbled up. I will have to sort them all out. I am hoping I can do that soon. I need to get back to some of my customers and my suppliers. I cannot hold up the construction projects. We are on deadlines," Sylvia explained.

"I can help her do the sorting if the adjuster will check them first, then go on to the other items," Jason said.

"Sure, I will ask him. We cannot hold up progress," Ray Larson said with a smile. "We will get all of this mess taken care of as soon as possible and let you get back to work. Do you have another office in the building you can use in the meantime?"

"She can use my office," stated Jason.

Sylvia looked at Jason and was eternally grateful that he was with her. She was not sure that she would be able to handle all of this without his support and his love. That was what really amazed her. He loved her, and she loved him in return. What a blessing for her. She was a little hesitant about staying with him, though. That pull to be together was pretty strong, but she did want to hold out for a while longer. She wasn't really scared, but cautious.

When the insurance adjuster indicated that he had completed his work in the office, Sylvia and Jason went in to see if they could make some sense of all the papers and files strewn over the floor. It looked like whoever did this vandalism knew that it would cause more trouble if the paper clips were removed from the papers and they were mixed up with other files. In doing the sorting, Jason seemed to find a pattern in the way the papers were tossed. It looked like someone stood at the desk and was tossing with both hands, one sheet of paper from a file to one side and another right behind it to the other side. After Jason figured this out, it made it fairly easy to pick up the papers and files and get them in the right order again.

Both Sylvia and Jason worked all afternoon phoning clients and suppliers and making sure that all was in order for each construction job that was active.

Sylvia worked for a while on some of the bids she was considering, and Jason made calls to his subcontractors working on a couple of the sites that seemed to be having some problems.

Sylvia still had no word on the bid acceptance for the off-site emergency room attached to Providence Hospital. There was only one week left until the winning contractor had to be notified one way or the other. She was really hoping that they would be the winning company. She had a crew that would be ready to start work on a new site in about two months. It would take that long to get the equipment and supplies ready to start preparing the ground for pouring of the foundations and doing the initial framework. The ground had yet to be cleared and graded, and that had to be finished before anything else could proceed.

Sylvia sat back to rest her eyes for a minute and was looking at Jason. He was a very good-looking man as well as being so nice and such a gentleman. When Roberta had called him, he was out on a job site, so his clothes were not the cleanest and his shoes were muddy. He usually cleaned up at the office at the sites before he came in to see her or work in his office. He had been in a hurry to get here when Roberta called. She loved him all the more for his haste to get to her.

"Are you ready to go get some supper, sweetheart?" Jason asked her in a soft voice.

"Sure. I am tired of battling all of this paperwork now. I need a fresh start in the morning," Sylvia answered.

"You know, tomorrow is Saturday. Do you want to go see if we can replace some of the furniture you will need?" Jason said. "I know some of the pieces were antiques. We could go searching in antique stores and see if we can find anything similar to the ones damaged."

"That sounds like fun. I would like to take some pictures of some of the pieces and see if we can find anyone who can restore them. I have a Polaroid camera in the office. We could use that to take the pictures," Sylvia said.

"Okay, good idea. Let's go by your house and pick up some clothes for you, take the pictures, then go to my place so I can clean up a bit. We can go to dinner, get home early, and be able to get an early start in the morning. If we can make some progress in finding some things that you like, then maybe I can help you with some more of the paperwork tomorrow afternoon," Jason proposed. "I really want you to get a good night's sleep. I can tell you haven't been sleeping very well. It shows in your eyes."

CHAPTER 16

Sylvia and Jason drove to the Sellwood Antique Area in Southeast Portland. It was not very far from Sylvia's house and had the largest concentration of antique stores in the area. They wandered into stores up one side of the street and down the other, but did not find anything of significance that would replace what she had. She did find a few small dishes that resembled ones that were broken, and she found two end tables that were similar to the ones smashed, but other than those items, they did not find anything that would replace some of the other larger items.

"I will probably have to purchase new items. I hate to have modern furniture in my house when there has always been vintage or antique, but I might not have a choice," mused Sylvia.

"I have a great idea. We can get some used furniture at a thrift store to hold you over until we can find the good antique stuff. Maybe we could take Saturday or Sunday mornings and go antiquing. It is fun wandering through the stores and seeing some of the stuff that people used to live with. Why don't you make a list of the items that you most want to replace with like kind, then we will know what we are looking for," explained Jason. He was excited about the prospect of shopping with her. This particular day had turned out to be fun, even though they didn't find much.

"Good idea! It will also be easier to know what I can spend on antiques when the insurance check comes in," said Sylvia.

Sylvia did not feel safe staying at the motel and decided to go ahead and stay at Jason's house, but felt very strange there. The temptation to sleep together was great for both of them, but she did not want to rush things. She wanted to make sure that their love for each other was the real thing and not just an infatuation. She had never really had a boyfriend before, and she didn't want to get hurt.

When Jason took her back to his place after their morning of hunting for furniture, she tried to tell him again how she felt.

"Jason, I did not have a very good role model in the relationship department. Look at my mother! She certainly is not what I want to become, and how do I know that I won't? She is the polar opposite of what I want to become, but I have her genes as well as my father's. How do I know that I will not become like her?" Sylvia asked with fear in her voice.

"I know you, sweetheart. You are not one thing like your mother. She is harsh and inconsiderate. She is a bully. She is not fit to have you as a daughter. Your personality is so much like your father's. He was kind and considerate of everyone he came in contact with. He cared about the people he worked with, and he cared about you, most of all," Jason explained to her. "When your dad hired me, he talked about you coming into the business when you finished your master's degree. And he talked about you inheriting the business someday. He said that he hoped I would stay on and work with you, that he thought we would make a good team."

"I am concerned about me being your boss. That must seem a little weird to you, working for a younger woman. If we are together, how is that going to look to the men who work for me?" Sylvia asked.

"When your dad was still alive, I used to think how it would be to marry the boss's daughter. Now I think about how it would be to marry the boss. I don't think the employees of Payne Construction would think twice about the fact that I would be married to the boss. They all think the world of you, and if we can maintain a professional attitude at work and around the employees, I do not see any problem," Jason commented.

"Marriage is a ways off. I want to get used to having you as a boyfriend first. I want you to know that I am still a virgin and I value that. Unlike my mother, I do not believe in sleeping around.

That is not to say that I will not sleep with you, but there has to be a mutual respect and understanding first," Sylvia stated firmly, but with a smile on her face.

"I understand, and you will never know how much I respect you for your feelings and for feeling free enough to share them with me. The only reason I think it is necessary for you to be here now is for your safety. Until they catch the person who is doing this vandalism, I don't think you are safe being alone. I figure your house will take about a week to clean up and make it livable. Are you going to replace the kitchen appliances that were damaged?" Jason asked.

"Yes. I do not want the dented and damaged appliances in my kitchen. I will go to Sears and purchase a new refrigerator, stove, and dishwasher. Fortunately, they did not go into the utility room, so the washer, dryer, and water heater are okay," explained Sylvia. "Will you contact the sub who does the tiling for us and see if he has someone he could spare to repair the tile in the master bathroom? The sledgehammer really did a job on it," asked Sylvia.

"I will ask him today. He is out at the strip-mall site now. He has just started his work there, but I am sure he can spare someone who can do the job. It will probably take at least a week before you will be able to use the shower. I also noticed that there was some damage to the brick fireplace. Do you use it a lot?" Jason asked her.

"Only in the winter months. It gets cold and damp, and the fire is always nice to take the chill off in the evening," Sylvia answered.

"The reason I asked is that we have a really excellent brick mason who does work for us when we need it. We sub the work out to him. He has his own masonry business," explained Jason.

"How about if I take you out to a nice dinner tonight and we forget about all of this and talk about pleasant subjects for a change?" asked a smiling Jason.

"Would it be a dinner that I could wear my new black dress?" asked Sylvia coyly.

"I suppose that I could make it into a dinner where you could wear a little black dress. I don't think I have ever seen you dressed in anything other than a business suit or jeans," Jason commented.

"I don't dress up very often. I bought this dress the day the house was vandalized. Shirley and I went on a shopping spree," Sylvia explained.

"Okay! A fancy dinner it is. Have you ever been to Genoa West?" Jason asked.

"No, I haven't. I have driven by it lots of times, but never eaten there. It looked too fancy for me," answered Sylvia.

"You go get ready, and I will call and make reservations. I happen to know someone who works there, so I will do my magic and you go do yours. I can't wait to see what your magic looks like," Jason said as he gave her a kiss on the cheek.

Sylvia went into the bedroom and pulled the dress out of the closet. She was going to take it back, thinking she would never wear it, so had not taken any of the tags off of it. She went into the bathroom to shower and fix her hair up in a bun at the nape of her neck.

Sylvia wore very little makeup but applied some for this evening. After putting the dress on and slipping her feet into her new black pumps, she felt pretty.

"Wow!" Jason said when Sylvia came out of her bedroom. "You look good enough to eat!"

"Thank you very much. You look pretty good dressed up too," Sylvia answered.

CHAPTER 17

Genoa West was located in the Belmont area of Southeast Portland and was one of the high-class restaurants in the area. Jason knew the owner, Michael Victor. He had done some construction work for him several years ago, and they had remained friends.

When Jason called to make a reservation, Michael happened to answer the reservation line. Jason was surprised to hear his voice, but knew that Michael would often work at the restaurant, doing whatever job needed to be done at the time. He had waited tables and even bussed tables when needed.

Jason knew that it was hard to get reservations at Genoa West at the last minute, but Michael said he would take care of everything, to come at 7:00, and his table would be ready for him.

When Jason and Sylvia walked into Genoa West, Michael was there to greet them and show them to their table. Jason had a big smile on his face when they approached their table and broke down and introduced Sylvia to Michael Victor, the owner of Genoa West.

Sylvia gave Jason a questioning look, and Michael explained that he and Jason were friends, that Jason had done some work for him several years ago, and they had remained good friends ever since.

"Enjoy your meal, Miss Payne. You have a top-notch friend here," Michael said as he shook Jason's hand and walked away to help some other customer.

Both Jason and Sylvia had a marvelous meal and were stuffed by the time they were ready to leave. They each had a glass of wine with their dinner but declined any dessert.

As Jason was pulling up to his house after the meal, he stopped the car at the end of his street, turned to Sylvia, and said, "I am going to give you something. I do not want you to take it wrong." He pulled out a beautiful ring from his coat pocket. It was a sapphire with two small diamonds on either side. "This was my mother's ring. I want you to have it as a promise ring. It is not an engagement ring. I do hope that someday I can give you an engagement ring, but in the meantime, I want you to know that I love you with all my heart and want to promise you my support, fidelity, and my love. Will you wear it?" asked Jason.

Sylvia had tears running down her face, probably ruining what makeup she did wear. "Yes, I will wear it. In turn, I will promise you my support, fidelity, and my love. I do hope that someday we can get married and have a family together, but I have to work on the business 100% now and do not want to obligate myself to marriage and raising a family. I really hope you understand, Jason."

"I do understand, sweetheart, and I will respect your decision," Jason assured her.

"I also want to make sure that you are okay with the idea of working for the boss. If we get married, it could cause some problems, not only personally but with the people we work with," Sylvia said, expressing her concern.

"I know several couples who work together. Maybe not the way we would, but I would make every effort to treat you as the boss during working hours. That does not mean I would not try to steal a kiss behind closed doors," Jason said jokingly as he gave her a peck on the cheek.

"Sweetheart, working together is something we will have to get used to and work on. During working hours, you will be the boss. Any other time, we will be equal partners."

"Okay! Let's just enjoy ourselves for the rest of the evening. I still feel funny about staying with you, but I guess it is the safest arrangement for now," Sylvia surmised.

Sylvia was honored that Jason would want to give her his mother's ring, but she wasn't sure she should wear it. People would think it was an engagement ring. "Thank you so much for this beautiful ring, but would you mind very much if I wore it on a chain around my neck? Since I have never worn a ring of any kind before, I am not sure that I would not damage it in some way."

"Of course not. You wear it any way you want to. Around your neck would be fine. Just as long as you know the significance behind it," answered Jason.

When Jason led Sylvia into his house, she went directly to the spare bedroom to change out of her black dress. She had a good time tonight, but didn't really feel comfortable wearing a dress as fancy as hers. She preferred to wear her business suits, a skirt and blouse, or better yet, slacks and a blouse and blazer. It was more her style.

The next morning, Sylvia was surprised at how well she had slept. She woke up at 7:00 AM to the smell of coffee brewing and the noise of Jason in the bathroom. She went to the kitchen and poured herself a cup of coffee. The morning newspaper was on the table, so she sat down to read it. She didn't really have the time to sit and read the paper like her father used to. He would read it from cover to cover every morning. But then, he woke up at 5:00 every morning. Sylvia liked to sleep in a little later. The idea of having coffee ready for her in the morning could become habit- forming, though.

As she turned the page of the paper to look for the funnies, she noticed her mother's picture on the society page. She did a double take when she saw her on the arm of Michael Victor, the owner of the restaurant where she and Jason ate last night. Geraldine looked like she was climbing all over him. Because of this, her mother would probably learn that she was out with Jason. God only knew what she would say about that. Sylvia was so angry, she almost went storming into Jason's bedroom but stopped herself in time.

When he opened his door, she was standing right there in front of him. "Did you know about this?" she demanded.

"What?" asked Jason, astounded that she would sound so angry after such a nice evening.

"Here, this newspaper article and picture," Sylvia said, shoving the paper in his face.

"Oh my God, no. I did not know about this. What in the hell is he thinking of, getting tangled up with Geraldine?" Jason roared. He walked over to the telephone and called Michael's private number. Michael answered the phone finally on the sixth ring with a mumbled "Hello."

"Did you know that the bimbo that is crawling all over you in the newspaper picture is Sylvia's mother? Did you tell her that we were at your restaurant last night?"

"What in the hell are you talking about, Jason? What picture and what newspaper and what bimbo? I go out with a lot of bimbos," Michael mumbled.

Jason heard him trying to silence someone in the background. "Is Geraldine Payne in bed with you, Michael?"

"None of your damn business, Jason!" Michael informed him.

"It is when it affects my boss and the business I work for. That woman has caused nothing but trouble for Sylvia for months now. Do yourself a favor, Michael, and get rid of her," Jason advised as he hung up the phone.

Sylvia was sitting on the sofa in tears at this latest development. "Now my mother will know about us and will make all kinds of embarrassing public comments. This is exactly what I did not want to happen."

"This is priceless," said Geraldine. "The newspapers will love the fact that my demented daughter, Sylvia Payne, is shacked up with her foreman, Jason Gorman. Michael, let me use the phone. I have to call the Oregonian and let them know the latest developments."

"What in the hell is going on, Geraldine? I had no idea you were old enough to have a daughter who was running a major company like Payne Construction."

Geraldine sputtered as she sat up on the edge of the bed. She was angry at Michael for saying what he did to her. "If you do not like what you see, there are plenty of others who do," she said as she got up, spun around to look at him, and grabbed her clothes off of the bed. "You can get up and get me home. We came here in your car, and I have no way to get back to my house."

"Take a cab!" Michael said with a surly voice. "I do not want to spend any more time with you than I have to."

CHAPTER 18

Sylvia and Jason were going to try to go to some more antique stores on Sunday, but she decided to go into the office and try to get some work done. She needed to get her mind off all the mess with her mother and needed to decide what her future might be with Jason.

She was scared that she would not be able to be married and keep the business at the top of its game. It seemed like it took so much work just to juggle all of the jobs that she wanted to do and keep all of her employees working and happy. If she and Jason were married, would she have enough time and energy to devote to both the business and her husband? And what if she had a baby?

Jason was disappointed when Sylvia left for the office. He was hoping to spend Sunday with her. He was also starting to wonder what life would be like if he was married to her. He was afraid that she would put the business as a priority and their marriage would come a distant second. He had to admit that idea was not one that agreed with him. He wanted a good solid marriage like his parents had, where they always came first in each other's eyes.

Sylvia worked for about three hours in the office, completing some orders and forms that had to be sent to suppliers. She reviewed some of the messages that Roberta had left on her desk, putting them in priority piles. After a while, she realized that she was just shuffling papers in an effort to avoid dealing with Jason and her mother.

Leaving the office, Sylvia decided to drive by her house and see what progress had been made on the cleanup. When she drove up, she opened the garage door and drove her car in. She closed the door and went into the house through the door from the garage. She did not want anyone to see that she was there. She walked out onto the back porch and looked at a very overgrown backyard. She hadn't done much to the yard since her father died, and the flower beds and trees were very overgrown. The lawn had been mowed, but that was about all. She felt bad about the condition of the yard. Her dad had always taken such good care of it and loved having the flower beds neat and tidy.

"Oh Daddy! I miss you so much," Sylvia cried. "Why did you have to leave me so soon? Mother is wreaking havoc with me and the business, and I don't know how much more I can take. Jason says he loves me and wants to get married someday. He even gave me a promise ring that belonged to his mother. I do love him, Daddy, but I am not sure that I can make a marriage and the business both work. I didn't really have a good model to follow with you and Mother."

Sylvia got up from the back step and went inside to call the gardener that her father used. "Mr. Storm, this is Sylvia Payne. I was wondering if you had some time to come and look at my yard. I'm afraid I have ignored the trees and flower beds since Daddy died, and they do need a lot of care."

"Sylvia, it is so good to hear from you. I was so sorry to learn of your daddy's passing. He was a good friend to me and my family. I would love to come and look at your yard. Would you have some time today? My wife is visiting our children in Seattle, and I am at loose ends on this Sunday afternoon," suggested Mr. Storm.

"Today would be great. I am here now. Anytime you can come over would be fine," Sylvia said.

"I will be over soon. And please call me Stormy, like your Papa did," Mr. Storm said.

Sylvia then called Jason to let him know where she was and tell him that Stormy was coming over to look at the yard and let her know what needed to be done. There was a message on Jason's answering machine that indicated that he was not home. She left a message for him and then went about straightening up some more rooms in her house.

Sylvia and Stormy worked a good portion of the afternoon in the yard. They did some cleanup work on the flower beds, and he made arrangements to spend at least two days a week getting the flower beds and the trees cleaned up and in pristine condition again.

After working in the house for a while, Sylvia sat down and made a list of just what she wanted to buy for the house and the precise order in which she wanted to buy them. First and foremost was a new bed and bedroom set. Hers had been smashed to bits, along with her father's set. She decided that she was going to move into the master bedroom and fix up her room as an office. For some reason, the vandals had not touched the guest bedroom, so it was still in livable condition. She wasn't sure why she didn't just move into that room instead of going to Jason's house for the duration of the repairs. She would let Jason know that she was going to move back home.

Just as she was starting to leave, Sylvia heard a car pull up in the driveway, blocking the garage door. She looked out the window and saw Jason getting out of his car with what looked like a pizza in his hands. She wasn't really ready for him yet, but she was hungry, and pizza sounded very good.

"Hi," Sylvia greeted him at the door. "I called and left a message on your machine to let you know I was here."

"I know, I heard it. That is why the pizza," Jason said as he handed her the box. "I'm glad you are okay. I was worried about you." He leaned over and gave her a brief kiss on the cheek.

"Thanks for the pizza. I was getting hungry. I must go to Sears and buy new appliances so I can stock up on some food. What I had in the refrigerator spoiled and had to be thrown out," commented Sylvia.

"Are you going to move back in here?" Jason tentatively asked.

"Yes. I think I will. I did not realize that the vandals did not bother with the guest bedroom and it is still livable. I will just move into it until I can get the master bedroom fixed to my liking. I will move into it instead of back into my old room," Sylvia explained.

"Will you feel safe here since the vandals have not been caught yet?" Jason asked.

"Yes! I am going to have added security installed on all of the windows as well as a new system at all of the doors, including the garage door. It will make the house like a fortress, but it apparently is the only way I can live for the time being, and I need to be in my own home. I know I don't have a lot of my old things around me, but what I do have will be mine, things that I chose myself," she stated firmly.

Jason had just pulled up to the garage when Sylvia drove in behind him. At this point, he was unsure as to their future. He loved her so much but wanted to respect her wishes to remain celibate for a while longer. Her emotions were in turmoil because of her mother and now the knowledge that their relationship might be fodder for the newspapers. It was hard enough for her to run the business without her father's guidance. Her confidence seemed to be ebbing with each new attack by her mother.

"Do you want to watch a movie or listen to some music?" Jason asked her when they went inside.

"No, I think I will just go to bed. I am really tired and need to get a good night's sleep so I can be ready for a busy day tomorrow," Sylvia commented. "I hope you understand. I am really not sure which direction I am going in right now. I do love you, though, and I want to have a future with you, but right now, I can't see how that is going to happen. I have to concentrate on work and keeping the business viable."

"I understand, sweetheart. I love you! Have a good night's sleep. If you need anything, please let me know," Jason said as he gave her a big hug.

CHAPTER 19

On Monday morning, Sylvia packed up the things that she had at Jason's house, put them in her car, and headed for her office. She had a busy day ahead of her with back-to-back appointments with subcontractors and suppliers. She needed to be on the top of her game with the new off-site emergency room that they were going to build. They were to break ground in a month, and she wanted to have all of her subs and suppliers on board before that happened. She didn't want any surprises at the last minute.

Jason had gone to one of the work sites to check up on a few minor problems that they were having. She called him at the construction site to ask if he could sit in on meetings with two of the subcontractors. She knew exactly what she wanted from them and how to approach them, but she was not sure whether they were comfortable taking orders from a female. They had both worked with her father for a long time and knew Sylvia, but were not sure that she knew what she was doing. She thought that her mother's comments in the newspaper had had some influence on them.

"I will be there for both of the meetings," Jason assured her. "I need to get these small problems settled, and then I will be coming in to the office."

"Thanks so much. I will explain why I want you here when you get in. If you could be a couple of minutes early, I would appreciate it," Sylvia explained.

"Okay!" Jason answered and hung up the phone.

Fortunately, the blueprints for the emergency room were not damaged when her office was vandalized. She had them locked in her safe along with the bid numbers. Today her first meeting was with the electrical contractor and his foreman, and her second meeting was with the plumber and his foreman. She needed to nail down their costs for supplies and equipment and make sure that they were within budget.

Both of the subcontractors that she hired had worked with her father and seemed to be somewhat reluctant to work with her. She wanted Jason there to reassure them that the company had not changed. It was still the same reliable business that it was when her father was alive and running it.

Sylvia was well aware of the fact that she did not have the experience working with men that her father had. She knew it wasn't for the reasons her mother spouted, but she was young and inexperienced where men were concerned. She was sure that they were hesitant in expressing their views in front of her. Jason's presence would help.

Sylvia's mind kept going back to Jason. She did love him, and she was realizing that she had loved him for a long time. The physical attraction was great, but so was the emotional attraction. They had a lot in common, and their views on life and family were so much alike.

She just couldn't get her head around the fact that she would be his boss. That was a really foreign concept to most men. And she did not want to give up control of Payne Construction. This was her father's legacy, and she wanted to continue running it in a manner that would make him proud. She was beginning to realize that Jason was going to be an important part of that goal, whether it be as her husband or as a trusted friend and colleague.

Roberta buzzed the intercom to let Sylvia know that Jason was waiting to see her. That statement from Roberta hit Sylvia. What would it be like if they were married and Jason had to wait in the outer office to be able to see her? All of these questions were rolling through her mind when Jason walked in.

"Hello!" he said with a softness in his voice that made Sylvia's heart melt.

"Hello. Thanks for coming in this morning. I have meetings with both Jeff Ranger from Ranger's Plumbing and Jon and James Powers of Powers Brothers Electric. Both companies have the sub bids on the emergency room. Dad worked with both firms and trusted them, but they have shown some hesitancy in working with me. I hate to admit it, but all three men can be intimidating. I am sure I can handle them, but I appreciate you being here as a backup," Sylvia explained.

"No problem. I am happy to sit in on the meetings," Jason said with a little surly tone to his voice.

"Jason, I want you to know that my feelings for you have not changed. Right now, I am so confused with all of this mess with my mother, and I am afraid it is eroding my confidence in being able to do this job. Please know that I do want a future with you, but right now, it is not my number one priority. Right now, I have to concentrate on getting this emergency room built and keeping my employees at work and happy," Sylvia explained.

Just then, Roberta buzzed Sylvia to let her know that Jeff Ranger was there to see her.

"Please show him in, Roberta. Thanks," said Sylvia.

"Good morning, Jeff," Sylvia stood and greeted Jeff Ranger with a firm handshake. "We have a lot to discuss this morning. I am glad you are on board with this project."

"I need to say something first," Jeff said. "I am here as a courtesy to your father's memory. I have heard rumors about Payne Construction and the fact that you are going to turn the company over to your mother, that you are leaving the business. Is this true? If it is, we will be backing out of the project. I already have concerns about working with a woman, especially such a young woman. If you were to come onto the job site, your presence would be a distraction to my men, and mistakes could be made or accidents could happen."

Sylvia turned beet red at his statements and was so mad, she could not speak for a few minutes. Jason spoke up and said, "Listen, Jeff. You and I have worked on a lot of projects together. You know that Payne Construction does top-quality work and is known for the fair treatment of their employees. Just because the owner of the business is a woman does not mean that her conduct is not completely professional. I am the company's Project Superintendent, which means that I am one step down from Miss Payne in the line of command. And trust me, she is not going to turn this company over to her mother or anyone else. She is one of the most capable persons I have ever met, male or female."

Sylvia looked up at Jason and couldn't have loved him more than she did at that moment. "I am sorry you have had concerns about me and about Payne Construction. Unfortunately, there have been rumors about me and about the company. They have all been started by my mother. I am not fond of airing dirty family secrets in public, but my mother is trying to do everything she can to get control of Payne Construction, including spreading nasty rumors about me and the health of the company. Please believe me when I say that I am not giving up control of Payne Construction. If you feel more comfortable working exclusively with Jason, that can be arranged. He has my complete confidence and has the authority to speak for me and for Payne Construction."

CHAPTER 20

Jeff Ranger was impressed with Sylvia's manner when she talked to him. He was ready to back out of the job because of the rumors going around about her and her ability to run the business. He did not want his business involved in the controversy if that happened. But now, he was doing some rethinking about the job. It would be a good, profitable job for his crew and for his business. He wanted the work. He had the job if he could adjust to working with a young girl. But Jason had vouched for her, and he really knew Payne Construction very well.

"Okay. We will accept working with you and Payne Construction.

You really seem like you know how to run this business," Jeff confirmed.

"What rumor did you have trouble with? I am curious," Sylvia asked.

"I heard a rumor that you had lied about your degree from Stanford. That bothered me. I figured that if you lied about something as important as that, you might lie about something that affected my business," Jeff explained.

"First of all, I do have a master's degree in business and marketing from Stanford. The rumor started because I did not participate in the actual graduation ceremony. My father had died the October before graduation, and I was still grieving for him and trying to learn how to run a business. If you would like to see my diploma, I will gladly show it to you," Sylvia said.

"No, that is not necessary. I believe you. How in the world did a rumor like that get started?" Jeff asked.

"My mother. She is trying very hard to take over Payne Construction. She has no income now since alimony payments stopped when my father died. If she does get control of the company, she will bleed it dry, and there will be nothing left. She is making a concerted effort to make me the bad guy in this whole mess. I am sorry that my subcontractors or anyone has to be subjected to this. I am trying very hard to run a successful business and continue my father's legacy as an honest and fair business owner in this community," explained Sylvia.

"At this time, from my point of view, you are doing a good job of fulfilling your father's dream. I and my company will continue to do business with Payne Construction, and I will let my friends in the business know that your company has not changed since Thomas Payne died," Jeff said with conviction.

"Thank you, Mr. Ranger. Shall we get down to the business of building this new off-site emergency center?"

"By all means!" Jeff said as he spread out his papers on the conference desk and started to tell Sylvia about his needs and about his employees who would be working on the job.

Both Jason and Sylvia were pleased with the outcome of the meeting with Ranger Plumbing. According to what Jeff laid out, the architects' plans were being followed to the correct specifications. Their next meeting was with both Jon and James Powers, owners of Powers Brothers Electric.

Rumor had it that Powers Brothers Electric was a hard company to work with. The brothers were young but very knowledgeable about their craft. Their main problem was that they did not get along with each other. They were estranged in their personal lives, but owned the business together, and neither one could afford, nor did they want to, buy the other out. Many of the large construction companies were not using them for their electrical work because of the tension and bitterness in the air.

When Powers Brothers won the bid for the electrical work on the emergency center, Jason advised Sylvia to be very careful in her acceptance of them. He said that the job sites that they were working on were not pleasant places to work. The brothers were always fighting, and it held up the other workers because decisions were not being made.

Sylvia took all of this information into consideration as both brothers walked into the conference room. Sylvia looked at Jason, gave him a small smile, and rose to shake both brothers' hands. She could tell there was animosity between them just by their body language and thought to herself, "This is going to be an interesting meeting."

Both she and Jason were surprised when the brothers both were concerned about Sylvia and Payne Construction being able to finish the job.

"We have heard rumors that you are going to sell the business. We are not eager to work for a company that will be going through a new owner transition while we are trying to get a major job finished," James Powers said.

"Where did you hear that I was selling Payne Construction?" Sylvia asked. She was demoralized that this subject was coming up again with another subcontractor. She had to waste her time and energy explaining her private life when she should be working on getting the job done.

"There have been rumors all over the construction business about Payne Construction being sold to Geraldine Rogers Payne, your mother. She is apparently saying that she will do a much better job of running the company than you are. Therefore, we are hesitant about taking on the job at this time," Jon Rogers explained.

Jason spoke up this time. "Let me set the record straight. Geraldine Rogers Payne, Sylvia Payne's mother, is not buying Payne Construction. If for some unknown reason she did get ahold of the company, she would either sell it and get the money, or she would run the company into the ground by bleeding all of the profit out of it. There would be no more Payne Construction."

Sylvia continued, "My mother has no money to buy me out, nor does she have the experience to run a company this large. I have been around Payne Construction all of my life. I have a master's degree in business and marketing and am fully capable of running this company. That does not mean that I will not make mistakes. Even the seasoned company owners make mistakes. But I am willing to try my hardest to make this company a positive legacy for my father," Sylvia informed the brothers.

"Okay!" the brothers said in unison as they opened their briefcases and got down to work. Sylvia was relieved that they were going to continue with the job. They might be difficult to work with, but they were the best, and that was what she wanted for this project.

Jason was equally happy about how both meetings went. It made his job a lot easier when the subs were on schedule and were happy with their environment. It made completing the job successfully when everyone was on board and on the same time schedule.

CHAPTER 21

All of the subcontractors that had won the bids for the off- site emergency center were going to proceed with the work. They had each talked to both Jeff Ranger and Jon and James Powers about the future of Payne Construction and were convinced that the company was sound and Sylvia was able to manage the construction company in the same manner that her father did.

Sylvia and Jason both were relieved that they were not going to lose the emergency center contract. Without the plumbing and electrical subcontractors, they would not have been able to build the center. It was too late to look for replacements.

Both Sylvia and Jason planned to be on hand for the groundbreaking. The Providence Hospital executives would certainly be there, and so would the press. This was a big and much-needed addition for North Portland. Sylvia just hoped that the publicity would be good for the company. Thanks to her mother, there had been enough bad press about her and about Payne Construction.

Every Fourth of July, Jason went to Lincoln City, Oregon, for the holiday. He and five of his friends from school would rent a house down there and have a male bonding weekend. July 4th happened to be on a

Friday this year, so he would be gone until Sunday evening. He always looked forward to getting together with his friends again and rehashing old times.

Sylvia had moved back into her house the last week in June, so she would be busy getting the house set up the way she wanted it again. The contractor had done a great job on repairing the structure, and she was able to have a few of the pieces of furniture professionally repaired, but she did need to replace quite a few items in the living and dining room. She had already bought a new bedroom set, so she had a place to sleep. She had her new bed moved into the master bedroom instead of her old bedroom. She was going to turn that into a home office for herself. The master bedroom had its own bathroom, so if she had visitors, she would not have to share.

She was working in the kitchen on Friday when the doorbell rang. She wiped her hands on the kitchen towel and went to the front door. She looked through the peephole to see who was there and recognized the man who was with her mother the day they tried to break into her house. His name was Darren Polk. She immediately went to the phone and called the police. She informed the dispatcher who was on her front porch, and Sylvia was told that a patrol car would be there shortly. The doorbell kept ringing. Sylvia was afraid the guy would give up and leave before the police got there, but just then, she heard a siren in the distance.

Darren must be an idiot. He must know that he was disobeying a court order to stay away from Sylvia and her home. He looked up when he heard the siren, but he just kept ringing the doorbell and knocking on the door, seemingly oblivious to the noise of the siren.

When the police officer approached Sylvia's house, Darren turned around and looked at them questioningly.

"Miss Payne's mother needs her. I am here to pick her up and take her to her mother. Her mother is sick," he said.

He talked like he was high on something. He just kept saying that Geraldine was sick and needed Sylvia. He was there to pick her up and take her to her mother.

The officer explained to Darren that he was under arrest for disobeying the court order, put him in handcuffs, then rang the doorbell again and announced himself as a City of Portland police officer.

Sylvia opened the door to see a very agitated Darren Polk standing there with his hands behind his back. He kept saying, "Your mother needs you. She is sick and needs your help. Please, she needs you!"

"Where is she?" asked Sylvia.

"She is in her apartment," Darren answered.

"If she is sick, why doesn't she go to the doctor or hospital emergency room? I have no desire to see my mother," Sylvia stated. "Thank you, officer, for coming so soon. I appreciate your quick response."

As Darren was being taken to the patrol car, Sylvia closed the door and set the alarm. Her alarm system was very sophisticated, allowing her to have an alarm set while she was inside the house and in the yard. She felt safer knowing no stranger could get into the house or backyard while she was there.

She continued to arrange her kitchen and bedroom the way she wanted them. She had done nothing about rearranging the kitchen after her father died. She had found it inconvenient when he was alive, but she said nothing to him. Now, she was able to arrange the cupboards the way she wanted them. Sylvia loved to cook, but did little of it. By putting the kitchen together the way she wanted, maybe it would inspire her to cook again. Most of the time now, she just warmed food up in the microwave oven or she went out and picked something up at a fast-food restaurant. She was thinking maybe she should cook a meal for Jason sometime.

Sylvia still had some mixed feelings about continuing a relationship with him. She so wanted to keep the business on a level that her father would approve of, but she also wanted a personal life. The thought of being alone was not one she liked to think about. Her experience in living in a family situation was limited. She was basically raised by her father. Would she know how to be a mother and work at the same time?

This business with her mother was really wearing on her. She did not know what would happen next, but somehow she had to stop the harassment. So far, she had been able to appease the subcontractors and let them know that Payne Construction was in good condition and could finish the jobs they had within the time limit with good quality work.

Even the fact that Ranger Plumbing and Powers Electric were hesitant about taking the jobs made her nervous. By having them question whether she could handle the job or not meant that they were listening to all the rumors and possibly believing some of them. Apparently, Geraldine's public harassment of her was having some effect.

CHAPTER 22

Sylvia sat on her back porch and watched what fireworks she could see the night of July 4th. She didn't like being alone, but this evening she did not have a choice. Shirley had a date with Justin for the whole weekend, and Jason was at the beach with all of his friends from school for their annual July 4th reunion. Sylvia hadn't kept up with any of her school friends, and none of them lived in the Portland area. Most of the friends she had at Stanford lived on the East Coast or in Southern California. She had no time to generate a lot of personal friends now. She was too busy working.

About 10:30 PM, Sylvia decided to go to bed. She was tired from working around the house, and tomorrow she wanted to work in the yard with Stormy. A good night's sleep was what she needed.

At 11:00 PM, her doorbell rang. She wasn't completely asleep, but the sound startled her, and she was afraid that her mother had sent someone else to harass her. She got up out of bed, put her robe on, and went to the front door and looked through the peephole to see who was there. She was startled to see Jason's face. What in the world was he doing there at this time of night? Maybe something was wrong.

Sylvia turned off the alarm and opened the door.

"I missed you!" Jason said meekly. "I didn't want to be away from you this weekend. All the guys talked about were their wives and kids. I felt like a complete outsider."

"Come in," Sylvia said quietly.

Jason walked in the door and took Sylvia into his arms. "I love you so much and do not want to be away from you. I want you with me all of the time," he murmured to her. Jason kissed her like he had never kissed her before, and she responded in kind. As they were kissing, they both were moving towards Sylvia's bedroom.

"I want you to stay with me, Jason," Sylvia murmured between kisses. "Are you sure?" Jason asked.

"Very sure. Just let me set the alarm. I had a visit from one of my mother's boyfriends earlier this evening and would not put it past my mother to send someone else to harass me," Sylvia explained.

Jason followed her to the door, looked out to make sure no one was there, and then she closed the door and set the alarm. He again took her into his arms and gave her a deep kiss, expressing his love for her.

As they were headed for the bedroom, Sylvia was helping Jason shed his jacket, shirt, and sandals. He was not wearing socks, just sandals, and his shorts came off easily. By the time they reached the bedroom, Sylvia had her bathrobe and nightgown off, and Jason just had his boxer shorts on. They fell onto the bed in each other's arms. Jason knew that Sylvia was a virgin and was very careful that he didn't hurt her too much, but the urge to plunge into her was so great, and she wanted him just as much.

They lay in each other's arms, totally spent, and both of them fell asleep. Sylvia woke up about an hour later and was surprised that she slept at all. She had never in her life slept with someone else in her bed. It was so easy with Jason. The moonlight was coming in through the open window, shining on his face. She gazed at him and pictured the rest of her life with him lying there. Would it work? I am his boss. Would he grow to resent me and my position at work? These were all things that she was thinking about when he woke up and gazed at her.

"Are you okay? You look worried. Did I hurt you when we made love? I tried to be as careful as I could," Jason said as he pulled her toward him again.

"No, you did not hurt me. You made me feel like I was the most special person in the world," she answered.

"You are!" Jason murmured to her and put his hand onto her breast. Sylvia immediately responded to the feel of his hand on her and moved even closer.

"I love you, Jason, and want you very much, but I am worried about where this is going to go. I do not want to be hurt if we can't make it together. Sure, we can make it physically. That is evident by the way we made love last night and the way I feel right now, but can we make it emotionally? I don't have very much history of living as a family. I only remember living with my dad, and even though he was so good to me and took excellent care of me, I missed having a mother to do the girly things with. My mother was more interested in traveling with her boyfriends than spending time with me," Sylvia stated firmly.

"Honey, we can make it emotionally. You are a strong person. I know you are worried about being my boss. I have no problem with that at all. You are so very capable of handling the business, and I am very conscious of you being the boss. If I do ever have a dispute with what you are doing, I will discuss it with you in private, and I will accept the fact that your decision is final. I feel that my love for you is strong enough to withstand any problems that we would have. I respect your ability to lead Payne Construction. I am happy being your company superintendent. The only thing that I would request is that when I come into your office and you are alone, I can kiss my boss," Jason asked with a grin on his face and his hand moving down her stomach.

Sylvia melted into his arms and moved her hands lower on his stomach as well.

When Jason and Sylvia finally got out of bed, they showered together, which took longer than a normal shower, got dressed, and went to the kitchen to make coffee and some scrambled eggs.

Sylvia needed to go to the grocery store and stock up on some basic items that she needed. She noticed that a lot of what her father had in his pantry was way out of date.

Jason had to go to his house to get some different clothes for the weekend, then offered to take her to the grocery and out to dinner that evening. Neither of them wanted anything fancy, just a place they could have a quiet dinner and talk.

During dinner, they talked about their living arrangements. Neither of them felt that they should live together all of the time. Sylvia did not want that to get out to her mother. It would just be more fodder for her mother to use against her. They did decide that they wanted to spend the weekends together. Sylvia was fixing up her old bedroom as a study for herself. She and Jason could both use it if they had to work on the weekends, which they often did when they were up against deadlines.

"I have enough room in my garage for you to park your car in there on the weekends. I guess I am becoming paranoid about having my mother knowing I am seeing anyone, and I don't want your name dragged through the mud. Mine is enough," Sylvia explained to Jason.

"Honey, I am not worried about your mother. I am strong enough to stand up to any of her antics, but I will park my car in your garage so you will feel better. I guess, after what has happened these past few months, you have a right to be uncomfortable. I just hope you are not uncomfortable having me around," Jason stated.

Sylvia cuddled up to him on the sofa. "I am not at all uncomfortable having you around. You make me feel something other than fear, anger, and sadness, and I will always thank you for that. I was beginning to think that I would never experience any other emotion."

Early Monday morning, Jason left to go to his house to get dressed for work. He did not take any work clothes to Sylvia's house. It was agreed that he would leave some of his things at her place so he didn't have to pack something every weekend, but he would not move in. He would still maintain his home and stay there during the work week.

CHAPTER 23

Roberta buzzed Sylvia on Monday morning, informing her that Jerome Browning was on the phone.

"Good morning, Jerry," Sylvia said with a lilt in her voice. She felt incredible this morning. "What can I do for you?"

"I have some not-so-good news for you. It's your mother again," her attorney said.

"What's she done now?" Sylvia asked hesitantly, not wanting her good mood to go away, but always ready for it to vanish when her mother was involved.

"Geraldine's attorney called me to let me know that she is going to bring an 'elder abuse' lawsuit against you," Jerry said.

"Good grief! What have I done now to get her hackles up, except not go with her jailbird boyfriend to, supposedly, 'take care' of her when she was sick? He was pounding on my door, and I called the police on him. He was violating the no-contact order," Sylvia explained to Jerry.

"Well, she is claiming that she was very sick and needed help and had no money to get to the hospital for care. She apparently fell and sprained her wrist and could not drive. Her attorney says she is asking for financial compensation for her pain and suffering and her inability to get medical attention as soon as she needed," Jerry announced.

"Unfortunately, she says she is going to make your lack of caring and concern for her public knowledge if you do not provide her some compensation. She wants a monthly income."

"You know, Jerry, I started out today in one of the best moods I have been in for months. Too bad it didn't even last half a day. What do I do now?" asked Sylvia.

"Well, hopefully, her attorney will be able to talk her out of this frivolous lawsuit, but if not, we wait for papers to be served and then answer them accordingly," Jerry said. "I just wanted you to have a heads up just in case you were served a summons today."

"Thanks, Jerry. Talk to you soon," Sylvia said as she hung up the receiver and put her head down on her desk and said to herself, "I don't deserve this. Why is she doing this to me? Maybe I should just give her some money and be done with it." But if she did give her money, she would have it spent in no time and would come back asking for more. She would never quit.

Sylvia buzzed Roberta and asked not to be disturbed for about an hour. She had some things to do and did not want to be interrupted. Then she sat and thought about her life and what it had become. This past weekend with Jason had shown her what her life could be like in the future, and she liked it. She liked the feeling of being a couple. She had never been part of a couple before.

All of a sudden, she knew what she was going to do. She called Jason at the emergency room construction site and asked him if he could come into the office. She had something important to talk to him about.

"Sure, it will take me about an hour to get there. I have to finish up with the cement guy, then I can come in. Are you okay?" Jason asked.

"Never better. See you soon," she answered. She buzzed Roberta to ask her to let Jason come in when he got there, but no one else.

Sylvia was still formulating in her mind what she wanted to say to Jason when Roberta led him into the office an hour later. She quietly closed the door behind her, wondering what was going on between those two and secretly hoping it was a budding romance.

Jason looked at Sylvia's serious face and said, "Hi, sweetheart. What's up?"

"I have a proposition for you. Please hear me out before you say anything. Jerry Browning called this morning to let me know that my mother is making threats of a lawsuit for elder abuse because of my lack of taking care of her. She wants me to give her a monthly amount of money, an allowance, I guess you could say. I will not do that. She will continually be coming back for more. I have another idea. I want you to marry me, and I will give you half of the company. That way she will not be able to get her hands on it," Sylvia announced with a grin on her face.

"What? You want me to marry you just so your mother will not get her hands on Payne Construction?" Jason said, astounded at what she had said.

"No, that's not the way I meant it. Let me explain. I felt happier this morning than I have in months. I have never been part of a couple before, and I felt like part of a couple this weekend. I love you so much, and I want this feeling to last. I do not want to lose you, ever. You are my first and only love," Sylvia explained. "I don't want to live with you only on the weekends. I want to be with you during the week also. I want to fix you dinners at night and cuddle up on the sofa and read a book or watch a TV show together. I am tired of being alone every evening."

"Oh, sweetheart. I want that too. I love you with all my heart, but are you sure you want to get married now?" he asked.

"Yes, I don't want to wait any longer. I am almost 27 years old, and it is time for me to grow up and become a wife," Sylvia stated. "But why give me half of your company?" Jason asked.

"You know, I have been concerned about the fact that if we were to marry, I would be your boss. I want us to be equal partners, not only in our marriage but in our work as well. Our basic jobs would not change. You are too good at what you do, and I would be hard pressed to replace you as construction superintendent, but you would have a vested interest in the company if you owned half of it," Sylvia explained. "It would also be nice to have some of the burden taken off of my shoulders for making all of the decisions."

"Yes, I will marry you. It is something I was going to ask you soon anyway. You just beat me to it, but I am not sure about you giving me half of your company. Your father worked very hard to build this company up, and for you to give up 50% control, well, I am not sure what he would think of that," Jason commented.

"Daddy loved you, Jason. He was so happy that you were a part of the company and was looking forward to a long association with you. Unfortunately, that did not happen for him, but I know he would be happy with my decision to give you half of the company," Sylvia said.

Both Jason and Sylvia stood in the middle of her office looking at each other and grinning. They gave each other a big hug and kiss then went out the office door to let Roberta know what was happening.

Roberta was thrilled at the news and started to cry. "Sylvia, I know that your father would be so pleased at this. I secretly thought that this was what he had in mind when he made Jason Construction Superintendent." She gave both of them a hug and shooed them out of the office to take the rest of the day off.

"Maybe we should go look at engagement rings," Jason said.

"I really do not want a diamond ring. I would prefer just a gold wedding ring, maybe one to match one that you would have," Sylvia said.

"Okay, when do you want to get married?" asked Jason. "Maybe next month?" Sylvia said questioningly.

"The sooner the better as far as I'm concerned," Jason said.

"I was thinking, if Stormy could get the backyard finished, we could be married there, unless you want a church wedding," Sylvia suggested.

"Your backyard would be perfect. It is so pretty and full of flowers. And August would be the peak of the summer flower season," Jason said.

CHAPTER 24

Sylvia's good friend Shirley would be her maid of honor. They went shopping for a wedding dress the weekend after Sylvia and Jason decided to get married. August 10th was the date chosen for the afternoon garden wedding. Because of the short time frame, generic invitations were sent out to only close friends and relatives.

After some lengthy and serious conversations, Geraldine's attorney had convinced her that she would lose any lawsuit she would file against her daughter for elder abuse. It would be a ridiculous claim, and she would be laughed out of court because of the antics she had already pulled and her constant harassment of her daughter.

Sylvia was very relieved to hear that there would be no lawsuit. She wanted the time to concentrate on her upcoming marriage, and she needed to continue to concentrate on her work.

Sylvia was excited about the dress she and Shirley found. It was an ivory-colored afternoon sleeveless dress with a full calf-length skirt. She would wear her hair up in a bun at the nape of her neck with a brimmed hat to match the dress. Her shoes were low-heeled, which would make it easier to walk in the grass in her backyard.

Jason decided to put his house up for sale. He saw no reason to keep it since Sylvia wanted to stay in her home. It was a much larger house than his and in a better part of the city. Jason didn't have much furniture that he wanted to keep. There were a few pieces that were his parents' and had some sentimental value, but most were not worth much. His kitchen was sparsely stocked with equipment, and none of it was very good. He had picked up most of what he had at garage sales or the Goodwill.

Sylvia suggested that he sell the house partially furnished. Jason thought that was a great idea, and it caused him less work in trying to get rid of all of the stuff.

Jason had an appraiser friend of his come in to appraise the house, and together they set a very fair price for the place. Within two weeks of listing the house, he had a very good offer on it. The buyers had been preapproved for a loan and asked for a quick closing.

So, the Saturday before they were married, Jason and Sylvia moved his stuff into her house. They piled boxes on one side of the garage and would wait until they got back from their honeymoon to unpack and sort through them.

In among all of the wedding planning, Sylvia was busy preparing a bid for a shopping mall in Canby, Oregon, 25 miles south of Portland on Highway 99 East. Canby is a great farming town with some of the best soils in the state. The shopping mall would not be a large one, but would add to the economy of the area with new businesses moving in. Sylvia wanted the contract for the construction. It would be a big boost to Payne Construction's bottom line.

Sylvia was working on the bidding process in her office the Tuesday before her wedding when Roberta buzzed her on the intercom to let her know that her mother was on the phone and wanted to talk to her.

"What does she want now?" Sylvia moaned. "I really don't have time for her, but I guess I had best talk to her."

"Yes, Mother. What can I do for you? I am very busy and do not have a lot of time to spare," Sylvia informed her mother.

"Why didn't you tell me that you were getting married? For God's sake, Sylvia, I am your mother. I should have been the first person you notified," Geraldine cried.

"Mother, you are not on the guest list. It is none of your business, and I do not want you at my wedding. If you try to show up, I will have the police take you away. There is still a no-contact order out against you. You are not to be anywhere near me, my home, or my office," Sylvia informed Geraldine very forcefully.

"Maybe Jason will have something to say about this," Geraldine whined. "I will be his mother-in-law. He will want me at your wedding."

"He and I both agreed that you were not going to be invited. Goodbye, Mother. I am very busy," Sylvia said as she hung up the phone. Now she just hoped that her mother would not try to cause any problems.

Sylvia managed to complete the bid for the shopping center and get it turned in before the deadline. It would be a couple of months before the winning bid was posted, so she had a little breathing space.

The work on the emergency room was proceeding ahead of schedule. The electrical and plumbing work had been completed, and the sheetrock was being put up now. As soon as that was finished, the finishing work would start with the floors being the first to be put down. There was a massive amount of tile to be installed, and it would take several weeks to get all of the floors tiled. Special lead- lined areas had to be built for the x-ray rooms, and a sophisticated telephone system was to be installed. Both Sylvia and Jason were pleased at the progress being made on the project.

On Friday, Sylvia took some time to visit the cemetery where her father was buried. She cried a little and told him about her love for Jason and her plans to give him half of Payne Construction. She hoped that her father would approve of her decision. She missed him terribly.

Saturday dawned bright and clear. The weather was to be in the low 80s with a very light breeze, perfect for an outdoor wedding. Stormy had done an incredible job of preparing the backyard. He had even taken on the job of setting up the chairs and canopy for the ceremony. He was so proud of Sylvia and proud of his work on the yard.

Sylvia, Shirley, and Roberta all went to the hairdresser in the morning, then came back to the house to get ready for the 1:00 PM ceremony. Jason had asked a Multnomah County judge to perform the ceremony for them. Neither one of them had a church affiliation and did not know a pastor to perform the ceremony. Cranford Flowers in the Sellwood area provided some additional flowers in pots around the yard and also decorated the canopy and arch where the actual ceremony would be held. Sylvia was to carry a bouquet of white and pink roses and carnations, and Shirley's bouquet would be pink and white carnations. Roberta was taking the place of the mother of the bride, much to Sylvia's relief.

As the time approached for Sylvia to walk down the makeshift aisle in her backyard, she was beginning to get a little nervous. She wanted everything to go off so nicely and without any trouble, but she was uncertain if her mother would try to come. Some of Jason's friends were on guard out front just in case she showed up. They would turn her away, or if she made a fuss, they would call the police. The officers who were stationed in the Sellwood precinct were getting to know Geraldine. They had responded to Sylvia's house several times these past few months.

At precisely 1:00 PM, the string quartet started playing. Roberta walked down the aisle to her seat in the front row, then Shirley walked down in a beautiful light blue day dress, perfect for the outdoor wedding. Then Sylvia proceeded down the aisle with her eyes only on Jason standing under the canopy of flowers. He was smiling and awestruck at how incredible she looked. As she approached him, he took her hand, leading her to stand beside him in front of their guests. Both of them chose to say the traditional vows to each other. A popular addition to the wedding ceremonies nowadays was for the bride and groom to write their own vows. Both Sylvia and Jason wanted to stick to the tradition of the judge having them repeat the vows to each other.

After Jason kissed Sylvia with gusto, the couple walked back up the aisle to clapping and cheering. Just before they stepped into the house, Jason again took Sylvia into his arms and gave her a big kiss. "I love you, Mrs. Gorman," he said to her.

"I love you, Mr. Gorman," she said to him.

CHAPTER 25

After a honeymoon in Victoria, BC, and a leisurely drive back down the Washington Coast, the newlyweds settled into a routine of working during the week and getting settled in Sylvia's house. It felt so good to have Jason there all of the time. She was not lonesome anymore and felt much more confident in herself now that she was married.

About a week after they returned from their honeymoon, Jerry Browning had the papers ready for both Sylvia and Jason to sign, giving half of Payne Construction to Jason. Although Jason was still hesitant about accepting 50% of the company, it was absolutely what Sylvia wanted, so he accepted it. For the first time, she signed her name on an official document: Sylvia Payne Gorman.

Payne Construction had won the bid to build the shopping center in Canby. Sylvia was pleased that she was able to keep her employees working with new projects. Both she and Jason were busy getting the details ironed out to start the build within the next two months. Hopefully, they would be able to get most of the exterior construction done before any bad weather set in.

Roberta buzzed Sylvia one Monday morning, two weeks after she and Jason returned from their honeymoon, saying that a newspaper reporter was on the line seeking clarification of a statement that her mother made to the press.

"Roberta, I do not have time to talk to the press now. Is it something to do with my mother?" asked Sylvia. "I believe so," replied Roberta.

"Okay, put them on," Sylvia said stoically. "This is Sylvia Gorman. What can I do for you?" she asked.

"This is Jennifer Parr from the Oregonian. I am trying to confirm a statement that your mother, Geraldine Rogers Payne, made regarding the dissolution of Payne Construction Company. She said you have given the company away. Is her statement true?" asked the reporter. "Your mother said that you were going to pass all of your current jobs off to other contractors."

"No, her statement is not true! She is fabricating lies about me and my company in order to intimidate me into giving her money. The truth is, when I married my husband, Jason Gorman, I signed 50% of the company over to him. He has been the project superintendent at Payne Construction for several years. My father hired him. He is very knowledgeable about the construction business and is a great asset to both Payne Construction and to me in being able to run a viable company. Our first priority will be to complete quality work in a timely manner for the people who put their trust in our expertise and to make sure that our employees are treated fairly and with respect," Sylvia stated firmly. "My husband is now an equal partner in Payne Construction and will assist me in making sure that our goals are met."

"But why would your mother make those statements if they are not true?" Miss Parr asked.

"My mother makes a career out of telling lies about me and about Payne Construction. She feels that, even though she was divorced from my father for several years before he died, she deserves to run Payne Construction. Unfortunately, if she did run it, the only thing she would do is run it into the ground. She knows nothing about running any kind of company. She has never worked and has no desire to," Sylvia answered. "I hope you will print my comments as I have told them to you. I want everyone to know that Payne Construction is alive and well and will continue to do business, only with two equal partners running the company now."

"Thank you, Mrs. Gorman," Jennifer Parr said as they both hung up their phones.

Sylvia sat at her desk thinking about everything that had happened to her since her dad died. There wasn't a day that passed by that she didn't think of him and miss his physical presence in her life. She had Jason with her now, but he was her husband, not her father. She missed Thomas' wise counsel, his sense of humor, and the caring concern he always had for her. She missed having a daddy.

When Sylvia was in school, she was always aware of her friends whose mothers would take them shopping, invite their friends over for sleepovers, and have tea parties with them. Her mother was never a presence in her life. She was in the house, but her mind was never on Sylvia. It was always on something that she wanted or was doing.

When Sylvia was eight years old, she remembered asking her mother if she could have two friends over for a sleepover. She had never had anyone to her house before. Her mother told her no, she could not have any of her friends there. Her mother told her that she didn't want any more dirty little people running around her house. One was enough. That was the time she started to disassociate herself from her mother.

What kind of mother would Sylvia make? Now that she was married to Jason, it was a distinct possibility that someday they would have a family. Without a good role model, would she make a good mother? Sylvia certainly hoped so.

"Stop daydreaming, Sylvia," she said to herself. "Get back to work." Sylvia got home before Jason did that Thursday evening. Labor

Day weekend was next week, and they had not discussed whether they were going to do anything special for the holiday. She sat down at the table and made a list of possible ideas. The roads would be crowded, and since it was the last holiday for kids before school started, she assumed that the beach and state parks would be jammed with tourists. Even though they would be busy, she put them on her list anyway. She also included a trip to Timberline Lodge, Multnomah Falls, Bonneville Dam, and maybe as far as The Dalles. Any of those would be a fun weekend outing. She had made quite a long list by the time Jason got home.

While Sylvia was in the kitchen fixing a salad for supper, Jason was looking at her list.

"What's this list, sweetheart?" asked Jason.

"Oh, I thought I would make a possible list of things to do and places to go for the Labor Day weekend," Sylvia answered.

"How about staying home for the weekend? We could have a nice quiet weekend with just the two of us, almost like extending our honeymoon, but at home. The roads will be crowded, and all of the resorts, state parks, and nice hotels will be full of tourists," Jason said.

"That is a perfect idea. Let's go to the grocery store and stock up on what we need for the weekend. Then we won't have to go out at all," Sylvia said with a wicked smile on her face.

CHAPTER 26

What Jason and Sylvia had hoped to be a quiet, peaceful holiday weekend at home turned out to be anything but. On Sunday morning at 2:30 AM, they received a phone call that there was a fire at a remodeling job they were doing in Gresham, Oregon. As a fill- in job, Sylvia often would bid on smaller remodeling jobs to keep her workers busy. They were not jobs that brought a lot of money into the company, but they were good jobs to keep a steady income for her employees. This particular job called for remodeling an old office building into one that would accommodate eight offices instead of two large ones. The work was about halfway complete when Sylvia got the phone call early on August 31st that a fire had engulfed the entire building within minutes.

Both Jason and Sylvia got dressed and headed for the job site. As they approached the street where the site was, they could see the flames and smoke and hear the sirens and the sound of the water being poured onto the building.

Jason always had a security guard posted at the job sites every night. When he couldn't find him, he asked a policeman if he had seen him. The officer pointed to the flaming building. "He's in there," he said. "We heard him yelling for help, but the building collapsed on him before we could get to him."

"Oh my God!" cried Sylvia. "He has a wife and two children."

George Chamberlin was one of the security guards that Payne Construction hired for their job sites. He was one of the few men who did not complain about working the graveyard shift.

When the firemen were finished getting the flames under control and the rescue workers could go into the building, George's body was brought out and put into an ambulance to be taken to the morgue. An autopsy would be performed, but it was obvious what had killed him.

Sylvia went into the construction shack where George had his personal things. His lunchbox and a book were sitting on the desk, but she noticed that the chair was overturned and some of the papers on the desk were in disarray. George was usually a very neat man, and it was odd that the room would look that way.

"Jason, would you come in here for a minute?" she hollered out the door at her husband. "Look at this room and tell me that it is out of character for George to leave it this way, even to make his rounds of the site."

Jason looked around the room and went out to call one of the remaining police officers into the shack. "George Chamberlin is one of the neatest workers that we have. I cannot imagine that he would leave his office area in this condition, even to make his rounds. He made rounds every 45 minutes. He would have straightened his desk before he left the shack. And why is this chair overturned? He must have heard something, or someone came in here," Jason told the officer.

"Let me get the fire chief in here to talk to you," the officer said. "We have called in the arson investigator. Two of my firemen

have found and smelled some evidence of an accelerant being used. If that is the case, this will be considered a homicide," the fire chief explained. "Please do not touch anything and leave everything the way it is. You can probably go home now. There is nothing that can be done at this point. The police will notify the next of kin. It is their job. His family will need you later on."

Jason and Sylvia drove home, stopping to get a cup of coffee on the way. When they got home, they plopped onto their sofa and just sat there. There was really nothing to be said at this point. They were still in shock. Who in the world would want to burn down a half-finished building, and who would want to hurt George Chamberlin, one of the nicest men and most loyal employees they knew?

Sylvia managed to get a couple of hours of sleep before she was interrupted by the phone ringing. Jason had gone outside to wander around in the backyard and try to make some sense of all of this. The hit on the company would not be huge. They did have insurance, but that was not the point. One of their valued employees had been killed. Jason could not get his mind around that.

Jason heard the phone ring, but he was too far away from the back door to get it before Sylvia did. He went into the bedroom to see who was on the phone.

Sylvia was as white as a sheet when he walked into the bedroom. "I answered the phone, and all I heard was a funny voice saying, 'serves you right.'" She had tears running down her face as Jason took her into his arms to give her what comfort he could.

"Did someone do this to get at us?" she looked up at her husband sadly. "I don't know, honey. I will call the fire chief that we talked to earlier. He will give the information to the arson investigator or to the police," Jason told her.

"I am going to take a shower, then I will fix us something to eat. I have a feeling that this will be a long day," Sylvia said sadly.

When Sylvia went into the bathroom, Jason walked out to the kitchen to check the backyard. He had forgotten to set the alarm when he came into the house to try and answer the phone before it woke Sylvia up. When he came back inside, he closed and locked the back door, made sure that the garage door was securely locked, and set the alarm. If someone was out to get them for some reason, he wanted to make sure that they were as safe as possible in their own home.

After he made sure the house was safe, he called a college friend of his who owned a security company. He wanted 24/7 security on the house and the office. He wasn't going to fool around with some idiot who wanted to hurt Sylvia.

Jason was on the phone with John Stevens when Sylvia came out of the bedroom. "Yes, John, I want that to start immediately. Send someone over as soon as you can. There is a credible threat against us, and I do not want to waste any time."

"What's up?" Sylvia asked.

"I have a college friend, John Stevens, who owns a security firm. I have ordered 24/7 security surveillance on our home and the office," explained Jason.

"Do you think that is really necessary?" asked Sylvia.

"Yes! I am not taking any chances with you. I want you around for a good long time. I am getting used to this living-together business. I want it to continue," Jason said as he put his arms around Sylvia and gave her a kiss on the forehead.

"Okay, but what do I do?" she asked.

"Just what you normally do. There will probably be two people watching the house and the office. John will come by today with two of his operatives to introduce them. He will explain the procedure to us. I just don't want you to be worried about our safety," Jason explained.

CHAPTER 27

The security guards were in place at both their home and at the office. Sylvia didn't notice them at the house. They were in their car most of the time. Several times a day, one of them would look into the backyard to make sure all was okay there, but on the whole, nothing was ever amiss. The guard at the office sat by the front door and watched everyone who came in. They all had to see Roberta before they could get in to see Sylvia or Jason if he was in the office. Most of the time, he was at the various job sites.

Bill Bowen was an arson investigator with the Multnomah County Fire District. He had been a fireman for 23 years when he applied for the position of arson investigator and was assigned to the East County area, which included Gresham, Oregon.

Bill determined that the fire was arson and that an accelerant was used to start it. When George Chamberlin noticed the flames, he ran into the building with the fire extinguisher from the construction shack. The fire was too big at that time. Apparently, a loose beam fell on him. He called out for help, but the smoke and fire were too advanced by the time the fire department got to him, and he died of smoke inhalation. The autopsy showed that he was not burned badly, but what killed him was the smoke.

Bill asked both Sylvia and Jason to review the news footage that was taken at the scene to see if they could recognize anyone.

Because Payne Construction had been in the news a lot lately, the reporters and cameramen were on site right after they heard about the fire. It was a big event in Gresham. The town was looking forward to having this expanded office building ready for tenants. It made sense that the better the building, the better the tenants, and the better the additional income would be for the City of Gresham. It was a win-win situation, and now it was all gone up in fire and smoke, and one person was dead. The future did not look as bright for the city tax revenue as it did before the fire.

Sylvia had gone over the footage a couple of times, each time recognizing no one in the crowd. Bill asked her to look once more, concentrating on the people in the background. As she was looking, she saw the figure of a man standing across the street, way in the back of the crowd. The man looked a little like Darren Polk, the man who was with her mother when they tried to break into her house. She told Bill about her suspicions and then wondered if her mother was involved in some way. Sylvia certainly hoped not. Even though Geraldine and Sylvia were not close, and Geraldine had caused her more trouble than she could figure, she was still her mother, and in some part of her heart, she supposed that she felt some affection for her.

"The man standing way in the back of the crowd in this picture looks a little like the man who tried to break into my home in late April. His name is Darren Polk. He was, or maybe still is, a friend of my mother's. He spent some time in jail for the attempted break-in," Sylvia explained to the officer.

"Thanks, I will check out his whereabouts the evening of the fire. I will also check out your mother's whereabouts," Bill told Sylvia.

"Did you find someone?" Jason asked when he walked up to the desk where she was sitting.

"Yeah! I think I saw my mother's friend Darren Polk in the background. Jason, what if my mother is involved in this? How do I handle that?" Sylvia cried. "I would really give anything right now for some peace and quiet. I don't know how much more I can take of this turmoil. Ever since Daddy died, there has been chaos in my life."

"We will get through it together, sweetheart," Jason said to her softly. "I will do everything that I can to keep us on an even keel. I love you so much and want to protect you from all of this, but realize that there is only so much I can do, but I will sure try."

Sylvia looked up at Jason and said very softly, "Thanks!"

In the days to come, Sylvia was in contact with the family of George Chamberlin to make sure they were okay and to make sure the funeral arrangements were being made to their satisfaction. Payne Construction had said that they would cover the cost of the funeral, so the family did not have to worry about any financial burden.

Two weeks after the fire and a week after George Chamberlin's funeral, Bill Bowen asked for an appointment with Sylvia and Jason at their home. On Monday, 9/15/80, the investigator rang the doorbell of the Gormans' home. The security guard had cleared him to come to the door.

Jason answered the door and guided Bill Bowen into the living room. Sylvia stood to shake his hand.

"I have some news for you regarding Darren Polk," he said. "Mr. Polk has a long rap sheet, and one of the crimes he was arrested for was arson. In fact, he was arrested three times for arson but was cleared every time. He has spent a lot of time in jail, but never for arson. We are looking for him at this time, but so far have not been able to find him. He has not been at any of his usual haunts for the last two weeks," he explained to Jason and Sylvia.

"What about my mother?" Sylvia asked with caution.

"Right now, your mother is on a cruise in the Bahamas. She is out of our reach. The cruise is a 30-day cruise with stops in many Caribbean ports. She boarded the boat in Fort Lauderdale, Florida, two days after the fire. At this point, we have no way of knowing if she was involved or not. And before you ask, no, Darren Polk is not with her. She is with some older man."

Sylvia mumbled under her breath, "Probably some other man she can wheedle money out of."

"My mother is the woman with 'a man in every port,' instead of the other way around. She cannot say no to anyone who has some money to spend on her," Sylvia explained to Bill. "She is getting less particular as she gets older. The money is what attracts her, not the man."

Bill, the seasoned firefighter and arson investigator, wondered how a daughter could be so cold towards her mother. He knew nothing of the history between the two of them.

"You need to read some of the articles in the Oregonian that Geraldine Rogers Payne had given interviews for. She has raked Sylvia up one side and down the other. Her comments have not been kind to her daughter," Jason explained. "Also, you might want to read some of the court documents regarding the lawsuits that have been filed by Geraldine. They can be eye-opening."

Bill looked at both Jason and Sylvia and said, "Do you think she could have had anything to do with the fire?"

"My mother is cold and callous and feels that she can do anything she wants to do, no matter what the law says or who it will hurt. She divorced my father but continually tried to reconcile with him, even though she had other men in her life. When they divorced, my father paid a very healthy alimony each month, which allowed her to travel and do pretty much what she wanted to do without the restraints of marriage and family. When my father died, that alimony payment stopped. She received no more money from the family or Payne Construction Company," Sylvia explained to the investigator. "She was livid when she found out that I had inherited the company and the house. Daddy left her the value of one of his life insurance policies, and if she would have been smart, she would have invested the money and had a good income for the rest of her life, but my mother has never been known as wise.

She went through that money like it was a bag of candy. That's when she realized that she would not get anything from me and started the campaign to take over Payne Construction."

"You have to understand, Geraldine never wanted to be a mother, and she did not take care of Sylvia when she was a baby. Thomas, Sylvia's father, took her to the office with him almost every day. He was both mother and father to this tiny baby, while Geraldine was off on a trip with one of her male friends," Jason added.

"I would hope that my mother did not have anything to do with this fire or the death of George Chamberlin, but I would not completely rule it out," Sylvia continued to explain sadly.

CHAPTER 28

The strain on Sylvia was beginning to show at work. She was short with Roberta and oftentimes snapped at her when it was not called for. Sylvia realized that she was not acting like her normal self, but there didn't seem to be much she could do about it. The fire and the death of George Chamberlin seemed to consume her thoughts. The thought that her mother could have anything to do with it was terrifying to her. What if she turned out to be like her mother?

Jason was getting very worried about her. He knew that she was concerned about the long-term viability of Payne Construction. He had never known her to have any doubts that she could run the company and be a good leader, but he was afraid she was having those thoughts now. All of the bad things that were happening were piling up on her, and he didn't know what to do about it.

Jason had started to take over more of the office work for Sylvia. There were times when he would ask her a question about a job or a problem with a supplier, and her response would be, "Do whatever you think is right, dear." That response really baffled him. She had never given up any of her responsibilities to anyone else.

Jason asked Roberta to come into his office one Wednesday morning. Sylvia didn't want to come to work that morning, but Jason, more or less, forced her to come. He didn't want her brooding at home all day.

"Roberta, would you be able to handle things for a couple of days? I want to take Sylvia away to the beach. The weather is still decent at Lincoln City, and I think a few days of relaxing and walking on the beach will be good for her."

"I will be fine. As long as the security is in place, there should be no problem. Until they catch this arsonist, everyone is a little on edge," Roberta stated.

"Thanks. You are a good friend as well as being a valued, beyond belief, employee of this company. I doubt if Sylvia will want to go, but I am going to shanghai her," Jason said with a grin on his face. "I will call you and let you know where we are staying. I am just going to play it by ear."

"Take good care of my girl. She certainly needs some downtime," Roberta said as she gave Jason a quick hug.

When he got home, he found Sylvia asleep on the sofa with the television running softly in the background. It looked like she had been watching some kind of game show. Jason decided to let her sleep for a while longer and went into their bedroom and pulled out two suitcases from the closet. He opened both of them on the bed and started putting some beach clothes in his. It was the middle of October, and the weather could be really nice or really awful, so he packed for both types of weather. He wasn't sure how long they would stay. He wanted to get Sylvia away from the stress of work for a few days at least.

Sylvia finally wandered into the bedroom and was surprised to see Jason packing a suitcase. "Did I do something wrong?" she asked with a shocked look on her face.

"Oh no, sweetheart. We are going to the beach. I want to get you away from the hassle around here for a few days. Roberta is going to take care of everything, and we have no urgent meetings or deadlines to meet for a couple of weeks. I got your suitcase down, but I don't know what you want to pack. You probably should pack for both good and bad weather. You can never tell at the beach this time of the year," Jason said. He wanted to be sure not to give her reason to refuse to pack her clothes.

"I don't think it is a good idea for us to be gone right now.

What if something happens?" asked Sylvia.

"Roberta will know where we are, and I have informed the security guard at both the office and here that if something comes up, to call her. She can get ahold of us if necessary. Honey, you need to get away from here and relax for a while. And, so do I. I want to walk on the beach with you and sleep with the smell of the ocean coming in the window," Jason stated firmly.

"Okay. The beach does sound like a good idea," Sylvia conceded.

"Hey, do you want to put the golf clubs in the car? The coast has some great courses. Have you ever played any of them?" Jason asked.

"No. Daddy and I never got around to playing anywhere but here in Portland. Mostly we played East Moreland, but occasionally we would play the Mt. Scott course. I have never played golf with you. It would be fun," Sylvia said.

Just as they were getting ready to leave the house, the phone rang. Jason contemplated not answering it, but then he did. It was Bill Bowen, the arson investigator.

"I just wanted to let you know that we have not found any sign of Darren Polk. He has not been seen by any of his cohorts since the day after the fire. We are still looking, but it doesn't look promising that we will find him anytime soon. As for Mrs. Payne, she is now in Acapulco. She doesn't seem to be in any hurry to get back. We will keep track of her though," Bill explained.

Jason thanked Bill and let him know what their plans were. "Roberta, Sylvia's secretary, will always know where we are and will be able to get ahold of us. We need this downtime. Things have been hectic since our wedding."

"Have a great time!" Bill said and hung up the phone. He envied the young couple. He wished he and his wife could take time off, but with three teenagers at home to keep an eagle eye on, they didn't feel like they could just leave to be by themselves.

Bill Bowen was a nice guy with a nasty job. Investigating arson fires was dirty work, both literally and figuratively. He hated the work, but he was good at ferreting out the arsonists, and he was persistent and kept at it until he had results. Bill and his wife were still deeply in love with each other after 17 years of marriage.

They had three children, two boys and a girl. Bill kept track of their activities all the time. He knew too well what could happen to kids if they didn't have parents who cared about them and kept up with their activities. Bill knew that sometimes his kids resented his interference in their activities, but they also often thanked him for caring about them enough to be concerned.

Bill admired both Sylvia and Jason, but most of all Sylvia for what she went through with her mother. He could not understand how Geraldine Payne could say such horrible and slanderous things about her own daughter. With everything that he had read about her, she was an upstanding businesswoman and ran a very successful business. He knew that her employees would do anything for her. That in itself said a lot. He was determined to find the person who set the fire in their building and caused the death of their employee. He wanted to do that for the Gormans.

CHAPTER 29

Sylvia was so glad that Jason had suggested the time at the beach and that they brought their golf clubs along. They drove to Seaside the first day and played nine holes at the Seaside golf course before they even checked into a motel.

"You are a good golfer, Jason," Sylvia said. "I'm surprised we haven't played together before."

"We were probably too busy. You are good too. Your dad did a good job of teaching you. That birdie you made on the third hole was outstanding," Jason complimented her.

The whole week they spent at the beach was so much fun. They played golf at every little course down the highway. They ate tons of seafood, stopped at Moe's for clam chowder in Lincoln City, and decided to keep going south.

They got up early to play a round of golf, then went back to their motel and back to bed. They made love with a passion that they didn't realize they had, then got up, showered, went out to get something to eat, and played another round of golf.

They drove as far as Newport, then decided that they had better turn around and go back home. They talked to Roberta every day, and so far, things were running smoothly, but they did not want to press their luck. They did have responsibilities.

They drove back up Interstate 5 to Portland. As they were driving down their street, they noticed several red lights flashing.

"Oh Lord, not again," moaned Sylvia. She looked at Jason's face and was very worried about him. He was as red as a beet from anger. She was afraid he would have a stroke or heart attack.

They had to park about a block away, and when they got out of the car, they ran up to their house. A Portland police officer stopped them from going any further.

"This is a crime scene; you can't go beyond this tape," he explained to them.

"This is our house. What happened?" Jason begged. Just then, Bill Bowen walked over to them and lifted the yellow tape for them to come in.

"What happened, Bill?" asked Sylvia.

"Apparently, Darren Polk showed up very early this morning. The security guard was doing his rounds, and Darren hit him over the head with the butt of his gun. Your neighbor, Mrs. Johnson, was awake and looking out her window when she saw it. She immediately called the police, and they came and caught Darren trying to break into your house. All of your alarms and whistles went off and scared him shitless. He started to run away, but realized that there was nowhere for him to go. He is on his way to the station as we speak," Bill explained.

"How is the guard? Was he badly hurt?" Sylvia asked.

"He's okay. He was not knocked out. He has a good-sized bump on his head, and the doc says for him to rest for a while as there is a slight concussion, but he will be fine," Bill explained.

"I hate to ask, but what about my mother? Any word on her?" asked Sylvia hesitantly.

"As far as we know, she is still in Mexico. She has a new man in her life who is spending bunches of bucks on her, so she probably isn't inclined to come home as long as he is in the picture," Bill told her.

"It is a relief that she is not involved in this," said Sylvia.

"We still don't know about any involvement she might have had in the fire. We cannot question her until she returns to the States," Bill explained. "I have a feeling that Darren Polk has gone rogue. I think he saw the potential for a big payoff here. He didn't know about your security or your neighbor with the good eyesight."

"I will go over and see Mrs. Johnson and let her know we are back and okay," Sylvia said as she started walking next door.

"Jason," Bill said, "I think Sylvia's mother is hip-deep in this mess. Polk kept saying, as he was being cuffed, that 'she said it would be easy.' He knew that you were out of town and the house was empty. He obviously didn't know about the guard. It really concerns me that he had a gun. He is a felon, and possession of a weapon is strictly forbidden. He will do serious jail time for that alone, not to mention attempted burglary, again. Who else would he have been talking about when he said it was an easy hit other than her mother?" Bill asked.

"Hell, I don't know! Please don't say anything to Sylvia if you don't have to. We had a good relaxing weekend. I don't want the chaos to start again right away. Let's let her think that it was Darren alone for a while at least," Jason asked.

"Yeah – I'll do what I can," said Bill.

Sylvia somehow knew that her mother was involved in this latest attempted break-in. Why would Darren do it if he wasn't prompted by her? She was not going to say anything to Jason about her feelings, though. She didn't want him to worry about her. They had just had such a fun week at the beach, and she fell more in love with him than she thought was possible.

On Monday morning, both Jason and Sylvia went in to work just like they normally would. They acted like nothing had happened, but a great vacation. Sylvia had a stack of phone messages to return and several files on her desk to attend to. The phone messages alone would keep her busy half the day. She had a great vacation, but it was good to be back to work.

Roberta filled her in on the progress of the jobs now being worked on. There had been no major problems, just some minor issues with a supplier who did not want to cooperate, but that was easily taken care of by the job foreman.

"It is getting to be the time to start thinking about the holiday party. It will take about a month to do the planning and get everything together. Do you have a theme in mind for this year?" Roberta asked her.

"I haven't even thought about it," Sylvia answered. "If you can think of a clever theme, go with it. I am not sure I am up to planning this year's party. Last year was hard because it was the first year Daddy was gone. This has not been an easy year for me. I have so much on my plate right now; a party is the last thing I want to plan. Could I impose on you to take care of it, Roberta? I would so much appreciate it."

"I will take care of everything," announced Roberta. "You don't need to worry about a thing."

CHAPTER 30

Darren Polk's arraignment for attempting to break into the Gormans' home was held Tuesday, October 28th. Both Jason and Sylvia attended the arraignment. They wanted to hear from Darren if Geraldine had anything to do with the break-in. But he said nothing at all at the arraignment. His public defender answered all of the necessary questions for him. Sylvia was disappointed that she still didn't know whether her mother was behind this incident.

They had gone to the arraignment in different cars. Sylvia had to go back to the office, and Jason was scheduled to visit all four of the construction sites they were working on. He also wanted to go out to Gresham and check on the cleanup of the property after the fire. The Gresham city council had decided to proceed with the construction of the shopping mall and still wanted Payne Construction to do the work. After Darren was arrested for trying to break into the Gormans' home, the investigation into the arson was geared up with him as the primary suspect. The property was finally cleared for cleanup at the first of November.

Sylvia was not feeling very well. She was lethargic and didn't want to eat. Even her morning coffee wasn't settling well on her stomach. She managed to get her work done, but was tired all of the time. Jason was so busy himself, he really did not notice that she wasn't eating very much or the fact that she went to bed by 8:00 PM almost every evening. By the time he got to bed at 10, she was sound asleep and didn't stir when he crawled under the covers.

All they seemed to talk about lately was either work or the upcoming trial of Darren Polk. They both would have to testify, and neither was looking forward to it. The only thing Sylvia was looking forward to was getting some answers about her mother's possible involvement.

Sylvia finally decided that she had better go to the doctor to see what was wrong with her. She was afraid she had cancer and was dying. She couldn't keep any food down at all and was beginning to be nauseous even looking at or smelling any type of food.

"Roberta, I have an appointment this afternoon at three. I will not be back in the office until tomorrow morning," Sylvia announced. "If Jason calls, please just tell him I am out and I will see him at home this evening."

Sylvia's doctor's office was not far from her office, so it only took her ten minutes to get there. She sat in her car for a few minutes, working up the courage to go in. She was afraid that something really serious was happening to her body and wasn't sure she wanted to know what it was.

"Hello, Mrs. Gorman. If you will sign in, I will get you back to an exam room right away. The doctor is with a patient right now, but will be with you shortly," the receptionist said.

"Thank you!" Sylvia mumbled.

The doctor's exam room was cold. She took off her clothes and put the gown on, but put her coat on over it. She was shivering cold. When Dr. David Martinson came in, he noticed that Sylvia was sitting there shivering. He opened the door and asked his nurse to get a warm blanket for Mrs. Gorman. When the nurse wrapped the warm blanket around Sylvia's shoulders, she felt much better. The nurse stayed in the room with the doctor and Sylvia.

After a lot of questions, some pushing and prodding on her stomach, a blood draw, and a very uncomfortable pelvic exam, the doctor left, and the nurse helped Sylvia get her clothes back on.

"Dr. Martinson will see you in his office, Mrs. Gorman." "Please have a seat, Sylvia. Are you feeling a little better?" he asked. "Yes. Thank you for the blanket. The room was very cold,"

Sylvia answered. "Is something seriously wrong with me? I think I might have some kind of stomach or colon cancer. I cannot seem to eat hardly anything," Sylvia tried to explain nervously.

"You do not have cancer, Sylvia. You are pregnant!" the doctor announced. "What?" Sylvia's eyes opened wide as her mouth fell open, and she stared at the doctor. "What did you say?"

"You are about six weeks pregnant," Dr. Martinson said again, with a big smile on his face. "Your baby will be born about the second week in June. I will be able to pinpoint a date more closely once the blood test is in."

Sylvia sat there with a stunned look on her face. The last thing she had thought about was that she could be pregnant. It did not even come up on her radar. She was convinced that she had a tumor and had cancer of some kind. "Pregnant," she whispered. "How in the world am I going to be a mother?" She certainly did not have a good role model to follow, Sylvia thought. "I don't know what to do with a baby. I have never been around them."

Sylvia was mumbling to herself. All of a sudden, she was more scared than when she thought she would die of cancer. "Dr. Martinson, my mother certainly was not a role model type mother. She never took care of me. I would doubt that she ever changed one of my diapers. My dad did all of that while mother was on a cruise or in some other exotic locale. I rarely saw her when I was a child. I have no idea how to be a mother," she stated matter-of-factly.

"There are classes at Emanuel Hospital that you can take. Both the mother and father attend classes. It will go over all of the basics of what to do for your baby. I have a feeling that the maternal instincts will appear as soon as you start to feel that baby move inside of you. I know your mother, and you are nothing like her. You are definitely your father's daughter," the doctor explained to her as he rose to lead her out of the office.

The nurse loaded her up with all kinds of brochures to look at and read, and a prescription for prenatal vitamins that she said must be taken daily.

When Sylvia walked into the house, she went directly to the den and put all of the brochures into a drawer in her desk. She did not want Jason to see them yet. She wanted to be able to tell him about the pregnancy in her own way. She wasn't sure she wanted to tell him at all. She was afraid. Afraid that she would not be a good mother. Afraid of not being able to manage the company and a family at the same time. And she was afraid that she would not know how to take care of a newborn baby. She had no friends with little children, so she couldn't ask anyone. Shirley was probably as clueless as she was.

Sylvia was asleep on the sofa when Jason got home from work that night. He had been at different job sites all day and was tired and dirty. He decided not to wake her but to go in and shower and change first. He wanted to talk to her about the possibility of her mother being involved in the arson and death of George Chamberlin. He wanted Sylvia to be prepared if Geraldine was found to be involved in either encouraging or hiring Darren to start the fire.

Sylvia walked into the bedroom as Jason was getting dressed. "Hi! When did you get home?" she asked.

"About 30 minutes ago. I needed a shower badly. I have been working at job sites all day and was pretty dirty and dusty," Jason explained.

"Any problems on any of the sites?" she asked.

"Nothing major. We have had a few minor delivery glitches with one of our flooring suppliers. On two of the sites, they have delivered a substandard quality product. It was not the product that we ordered. I need to do a little investigation, but I think they are shipping a product that is less expensive than what we ordered so that their profit margin will be higher. I will check it out, but in the meantime, all of the substandard flooring has to be ripped out and what we ordered has to be shipped and installed. That occurred on two of our job sites. I will do some research and see if I can find a new flooring supplier that will charge us a fair price.

"Thanks for taking care of all of this for me. I couldn't run this business without you. You are my rock," Sylvia said as she went to him to give him a hug.

Jason put his arms around her and gave her a kiss on the forehead. "I love you, sweetie. I am here to help you continue to make this business a success. We will always have a few glitches, but on the whole, the business is doing very well. I need to talk to you about Darren's trial," he mentioned.

"Ugh! I have been trying to forget about that," Sylvia moaned.

"I know, but I want you to be prepared mentally for the fact that evidence might come out that your mother was somehow involved. I don't want you to be caught off guard," Jason explained.

"I know that she could be involved. I have been thinking about it a lot lately. I hope she isn't, but I would not put it past her," Sylvia said.

CHAPTER 31

Darren Polk's trial for arson and manslaughter was postponed until February 1971. Sylvia was relieved that she would not have to be in the courtroom before Christmas, but she was not happy to prolong the suspense about whether her mother was involved.

Even though Bill Bowen's job as arson investigator was over, he still kept Jason and Sylvia up to date on the whereabouts of Geraldine, and as far as he could tell, she was still in Mexico with her new boyfriend. She was probably having a very good time spending his money.

The Payne Construction holiday party was being planned by Roberta Robinson. Last year's party was not really a party. It had only been two months since Thomas Payne had died, and everyone was still in shock and mourning. Sylvia did her best to make the party a happy, joyful time, but it was a miserable failure.

Roberta was working very hard to make this year's event a party for all of the employees. She had rented the Oaks Park Roller Rink in the Sellwood area of Southeast Portland for Saturday, December 13th, and chose the theme of "Santa Claus is Coming to Town." With Sylvia's permission, the party was going to put more emphasis on the children of their employees. Santa would be there with a bag full of toys for the kids.

Sylvia was very happy with the idea of not having a formal evening party for adults only. The entire company needed the joy of seeing excited children having fun.

Jason still didn't know that Sylvia was pregnant. She would have to tell him soon. She wasn't sure how he would feel, but he did have the right to know.

She left work early on Wednesday, November 19th, planning to fix Jason his favorite clam chowder for dinner and tell him then.

"What's the occasion?" Jason asked as he peered into the soup pot when he got home from work.

"I thought you would like a nice meal here at home. We both have been so busy the past few weeks. A relaxing evening sounded good," Sylvia explained.

"Are you finally going to tell me that you are going to have my baby?" asked Jason.

Sylvia stood in the kitchen with a stunned look on her face.

"How did you know?" she whispered.

"Sweetheart, I am married to you. I know your body like the back of my hand. Your body is changing. Your breasts are fuller, your waist is getting a little larger, and you have been sick in the mornings. Those are the classic signs of a pregnant woman," Jason explained.

"I didn't know if you wanted to have a baby. I was scared to tell you," Sylvia cried. "I am scared to death. I have no experience with babies at all, and I did not have such a great role model for motherhood. I don't ever remember even holding a baby. How in the world can I be a mother if I don't know how to be a mother?"

"Sweetheart, we will figure it out together," Jason assured her. Sylvia was relieved that Jason knew about the baby, but she was still scared to death. "The doctor gave me all kinds of brochures and pamphlets about classes I can take to learn how to handle a baby. I put them in my desk drawer. I really didn't want to think about it, but it is a reality, and I have to be realistic. We are going to have a baby. The doctor said he would be able to pinpoint the due date more closely when the blood test is in, but it would be about the second week in June."

"I wish I would have known that you were going to the doctor.

I would have gone with you," said Jason.

"I had no idea I was pregnant. I thought I had the stomach flu.

I was so lethargic and sick to my stomach; I went to the doctor.

I'm sorry I didn't say anything. You have been so busy, and I decided to see the doctor at the last minute. When I called his office for an appointment, I thought I would have to wait, but he had time for me right away," replied Sylvia.

"I would really like to go to your appointments with you when possible. Do you mind if I do?" asked Jason.

"No, I don't mind. I will probably have one more appointment with Dr. Martinson, then he will refer me to an obstetrician. He is the one who will see me through the rest of the pregnancy," Sylvia answered.

"I would like to keep this quiet for a while if you don't mind. I have to wrap my head around the idea of being pregnant before everyone else bombards me with questions and advice," Sylvia said with a questioning look on her face. "Do you mind?"

"I don't mind as long as you are comfortable with it. Don't you want to let Roberta know?" Jason inquired. "She has been such a good friend to both of us. It seems a shame not to share this kind of news with her."

"Okay. You are right. She will get worried if a doctor starts calling me. Will you go into the office with me tomorrow, and we will tell her together?" Sylvia asked.

"It's a plan!" Jason said as he took her in his arms again.

Roberta was busy with the last-minute details of the company Christmas party when Sylvia buzzed her and asked her to come into her office. Roberta came in with her pad in hand, ready to take down whatever instructions Sylvia had for her.

"Roberta, we have something to tell you," Jason said. Roberta looked at him with a worried look on her face. "What's wrong? Is somebody sick?" she inquired. "No. I am pregnant!" Sylvia stated firmly.

"Oh! Oh! I am so excited for you. What a great Christmas present. When are you due?" Roberta asked as she jumped up from her chair and gave both Sylvia and Jason a big hug.

"Sometime in the middle of June. Dr. Martinson says that I need to go to an OB doctor to find out for sure," Sylvia explained. She was glad Roberta was excited. She would need her support during this whole pregnancy. Roberta was more like a mother to her.

"I am going to excuse myself and get to work. I am needed at the emergency room site. I will see you later," Jason said to Sylvia as he gave her a kiss on the cheek. "Thanks, Roberta, for taking care of my girl."

"You are most welcome, Daddy!" Roberta answered with a grin on her face.

"How are the plans for the party coming along?" Sylvia inquired. "Great! There will be a sleigh come out at the end with Santa and a ton of gifts for the kids. We counted the number of children each employee had, and it came to 52, almost evenly divided between boys and girls. I had a team go out and purchase gifts for all of them, and they have all been wrapped. They will be in two different large red bags with either 'boy' or 'girl' marked on the gift," Roberta explained. "The people who run the skating rink will already have the rink decorated for the holidays. The dining room will be transformed into a winter wonderland for our afternoon meal. The whole thing should end about 5:30 or 6:00. I am hoping for a fun evening for everyone. This has been a stressful year for the employees as well as us. They need to have a fun time."

"Please allow about 30 minutes in the schedule for me to talk to the group," Sylvia mentioned.

"It's already scheduled right before we eat," Roberta said. "You sit down and take it easy. You look exhausted."

"I am much better than I was. I am scared to death of having a baby. Not so much actually giving birth to it, but the idea of caring for a baby terrifies me. I have never had a role model for a good mother. What if I am like my mother?" Sylvia asked Roberta in tears.

"You are nothing like your mother. You are your father through and through. And he took marvelous care of you. He had no idea how to care for a child either, but he learned, and he took excellent care of you. And don't worry. I will be here to help too. Sylvia, I love you like the daughter I didn't have. My sons were the best, but I always kind of thought of you as my daughter. So, I am always here to help," Roberta said while giving Sylvia a big hug.

"You are the best. Thank you! Now, let's see about the messages on my desk," Sylvia said as she sat down and looked at the stack of pink message slips.

CHAPTER 32

Jason arrived at the emergency room job site just in time to hear the conversation between the foreman and the flooring supplier. Apparently, the flooring that they had sent was not what was ordered. It was of substandard quality, and the foreman would not sign off on the shipment.

Jason arrived in time to intercede before a brawl broke out between the two men. The foreman would not sign for the shipment, and the driver would not leave without the signature.

Jason settled the issue by telling the driver to have his boss either replace the flooring with what was on the original order or Payne Construction was through doing business with them.

The driver gave Jason and the foreman a dirty look, turned around, and got into his truck to drive away. He would be in real trouble with his boss over this. His boss told him in no uncertain terms to leave this delivery at the job site.

"Have you dealt with that driver before on other sites?" Jason asked the foreman.

"No. He is new. That particular flooring company usually has the same two men deliver, but they were apparently not available today," the foreman responded.

"I will get to the bottom of this," said Jason. He spent some time talking to the other workmen, then got in his car and drove back to the office.

Sylvia had looked through the messages and saw one from Bill Bowen, the arson investigator on the Gresham shopping center fire. She knew that Darren Polk's trial was postponed until January and wondered what Bill wanted.

She picked up her phone to call him when Jason walked into her office. She raised her hand to have him wait just as Bill answered. "Hello Bill. This is Sylvia Gorman. I am returning your call."

"Your mother is back in town," Bill told her bluntly. "We received word from our investigator that she and her boyfriend arrived yesterday and are staying at the Hilton downtown. She has not returned to her apartment. I just wanted to let you know that she was back and that you might receive a call from her. We do know that her friend is a millionaire oilman from Oklahoma. They have been together for several months now and have been living the high life in Mexico."

Sylvia sighed as she said, "Thanks for the update, Bill. Is she going to be questioned about any role she might have played in the arson and death of George Chamberlin?"

"Absolutely!" Bill answered. "We will be picking her up today and taking her down to the station. She is a person of interest in the case, and we will question her in depth. Polk's attorney also wants to question her. He has her listed as a witness for the defense and needs to talk to her before the trial next month."

"Okay. Jason and I will be on the alert. She is liable to be super mad after talking to you. I will expect a call. Can you tell me if the 'no contact' order is still in effect?" she asked.

"As far as I know, it has never been rescinded, so yes, it is still in effect for both your office and your home," Bill answered her.

"Thanks, Bill. Talk to you later," Sylvia said as she hung up the phone and looked at Jason.

"You heard?" she asked.

"Yes. Is she back?" Jason asked in return.

"Yes. She's apparently staying at the Hilton with her boyfriend from Oklahoma. He is a big millionaire oilman. Bill said that she will be picked up today and taken to the police station for questioning about the arson and death of George. Apparently, Darren Polk's attorney has her on his witness list and wants to talk to her also. This could get very nasty," Sylvia said as she looked at her husband.

"I will stay close. I do not want to take a chance of her coming to either the office or house and confronting you without me near," Jason emphasized. "Are you going to tell her about the baby?"

"Not yet. I want to see what happens with the trial. She will know soon enough. It will be obvious soon. I am only in the first trimester, and I already feel like I am getting bigger. You probably will be repulsed by me when I am farther along," Sylvia bemoaned.

"Don't be silly," Jason said as he took her in his arms. "You, my sweet, are the most beautiful person in the world, and you will be even more beautiful as you grow bigger with my child."

Sylvia kissed him quickly and said, "We need to act professional in the office," she giggled. She moved to her desk, and Jason winked at her and went into his office.

About an hour later, Sylvia was reading some contracts she had to sign for a job she successfully bid on. The job would not start until April of 1971, but the owners wanted all of the paperwork taken care of before the start time. The owners were three men who had been running a successful investment business out of one of the men's basements. They were ready to have their own office and opted to have a new build instead of purchasing something that might need a remodel to fit their needs.

As she was about ready to sign the contract and get it ready for Jason to sign, Roberta buzzed her to tell her that her mother was on the line. Sylvia groaned and said,

"I guess I had best talk to her. She will just get pissed if I don't and try to see me here or at home. Please, no word about the baby, Roberta," she asked.

"Absolutely not!" Roberta answered.

Sylvia picked up the phone reluctantly and said, "Hello, Mother." "Hello, my darling daughter," Geraldine gushed. "How is married life?"

"I do not have time to chit-chat, Mother. What is it you want?" she asked.

"That's a little rude, Sylvia," Geraldine stated. "I haven't seen or talked to you in a while and wanted to catch up."

"Mother, we have nothing to catch up on. I have no interest at all in your activities or your new friends. I am really busy right now and do not have time to talk to you. Goodbye, Mother," Sylvia said as she hung up the phone.

She breathed a sigh of relief. She certainly hoped her child would not treat her the way she just treated her mother, but then Sylvia hoped that she would never give her child cause to treat her like that.

The Thanksgiving holiday was a quiet one for Jason and Sylvia. Roberta had them over for dinner, and the rest of the weekend was spent quietly at home. They slept late, cooked their meals together, watched a couple of movies on TV, and read. They tried to avoid any work-related activities or thoughts of Geraldine. On Sunday, they did venture out to buy a Christmas tree. They were anxious to have their first Christmas together. Sylvia had all of the decorations from her childhood, and she was eager to decorate the house. Then she realized that maybe Jason had some things that he would like to put out also.

"My dad wasn't keen on decorating for holidays, even Christmas. We had a tree, but he would put it up on Christmas Eve and take it down the day after Christmas. Mom always tried to have a present under the tree for me, but he wouldn't always let her buy something. He felt extras were not necessary. She would make special cookies and try to have a nice dinner for Christmas Day, but that was about the extent of our holiday celebration," Jason explained.

"Daddy tried to make the holiday as joyous as he could, especially because Mother was hardly ever here. She was usually off on some trip with friends. Do you mind me putting all of my stuff out?" Sylvia asked.

"Heaven's no! I am looking forward to having a joyous Christmas," Jason answered. "It's been a long time since I have had one."

Sylvia had fun decorating the house this year. Last year was so sad without her father there, and she didn't feel like putting a lot of decorations up. But this year was different. She still missed her father terribly, but she had Jason with her now, and she had a lot of reasons to be thankful this holiday season.

CHAPTER 33

The Payne Construction Christmas party was a huge success, especially with the children. Santa made his appearance on a pair of roller skates, taking a couple of turns around the rink before settling in his chair to talk to all of the children and pass out presents to them. Jason gave each of the employees a red envelope with their Christmas present inside. Even with all of the strife of the year, the company had done well, and the employees' bonuses were generous.

Sylvia looked radiant in a new red dress Jason had purchased for the occasion. It fit her perfectly and gave no hint of her pregnancy. She opted not to take a turn around the roller rink; she certainly did not want to fall.

The only glitch in the whole day was that Geraldine and her millionaire boyfriend tried to get into the party. The security guards were on alert, and they were not allowed to enter. Geraldine was incensed that she was not allowed to go to the party. After all, she was a Payne.

Geraldine's boyfriend tried to use his influence to get into the party, but he had no luck. The security guard was insistent that they leave.

Jason and Sylvia heard about the incident after the party broke up. Sylvia figured that the Oaks Park Roller Rink was not on the list of places that Geraldine could not go.

They were not going to worry about Geraldine at this time but were going to stay alert. With Darren behind bars, they were not too worried about any violence. Geraldine's boyfriend was an unknown, though.

Bill Bowen had told them that his name was Luke Gregson and that he was in his 60s. He was from Tulsa, OK, and had struck oil on his property in the early 1960s. He was spending his money about as fast as it was coming out of the ground. Geraldine was the recipient of much of his generosity. He had apparently offered the security guard at the roller rink money to let them into the Christmas party.

Both Jason and Sylvia were glad to know what they were up against, but they were not really worried about the company. It was on solid ground, and the last run of attacks that Geraldine made did not work, so if she tried that again, they were ready to counteract the lies.

Right now, all they wanted to concentrate on was their first Christmas together. Sylvia had purchased Jason a beautiful leather jacket for work. She had also bought him a really nice brown leather briefcase to use. He had been setting the loose files in the car. She had a lot of other small gifts for him as well. She and Shirley had a great day shopping for Christmas gifts for everyone.

Shirley and her boyfriend Justin Howard were going to join Jason and Sylvia for the holiday dinner. Sylvia was looking forward to cooking. She had not yet told Shirley that she was pregnant, so it would be a surprise at dinner on Christmas Day.

Roberta was taking a few days off and going to her sister's house in Seattle. She and Sylvia had exchanged gifts before she left. Roberta received her Christmas bonus at the party, with a little something extra added in for her work on organizing the party, but Sylvia had a little trinket for her anyway.

Jason wasn't sure what to give Sylvia for Christmas, but he found a beautiful diamond necklace at a jewelry store in Southeast Portland called Stookey's. It was a small store, and Mr. Stookey designed and created a lot of his own pieces. Jason talked to him about the necklace. It was in the shape of a heart and had 10 small diamonds around the outside and one larger one hanging inside the heart. Jason thought it would be perfect for Sylvia.

On Christmas Eve, Jason and Sylvia went to a candlelight church service at the Sellwood Methodist Church and then went home. It was a cold, windy evening, and the weatherman was predicting a rainy Christmas Day. It was a good day to stay home, build a fire, and cuddle on the sofa, but Sylvia and Jason had invited Shirley and her boyfriend over for dinner, so she had to cook. About 10 AM on Christmas Day, Shirley called to tell Sylvia that Justin had been in a car accident the night before. He was okay but had a broken ankle, and they would not be able to come for dinner.

Sylvia had not started cooking dinner yet, and they decided to have a very simple dinner of tomato soup and grilled cheese sandwiches. They were happy to be by themselves on this day.

They were both engrossed in their books when the doorbell rang. They had dismissed the security guard for the dinner hour so that he could spend the time with his family. He was due back in about a half hour.

Jason got up to answer the door. Fortunately, he looked out the peephole before opening the door. He also did not turn the alarm off yet, so he felt pretty safe. He did not recognize the man standing there. He was probably in his 60s, was fairly tall, and had grey hair.

Jason left the security latch on the door and opened it very slowly. "What can I do for you?" Jason asked.

"My name is Luke Gregson. I am a friend of Geraldine Payne.

She would like to see her daughter," Luke explained.

"You tell Mrs. Payne that her daughter does not want to see her and that she is violating a protective order by being on this property. If you are not off the property immediately, I will call the police and have Mrs. Payne arrested again," Jason announced.

"Seems like you could make an exception. After all, it is Christmas," Gregson said.

"No exceptions!" answered Jason as he closed the door.

Luke Gregson just stood there looking at the door. He was not used to having anyone close a door on him or not doing what he asked. He rang the doorbell again. He was appalled that Sylvia would refuse to see her mother on Christmas. No one answered.

Luke finally went back to his car where Geraldine was waiting. "She will not see you," he said. "Her husband mentioned something about a no-contact order still being in effect and you were not allowed within so many feet of her property."

"What a bitch! She is an ungrateful daughter. Not even wanting to see her mother at Christmas time. Let's go, my darling. Now I do not want to see her. I will deal with her later. I had thought this problem was taken care of months ago," Geraldine expounded.

"I am in the mood for a good steak. Do you know any good steakhouses in the area?" Luke asked.

"I sure do. It's called The Old Country Kitchen, and they serve a 72 oz. steak there. It is one of the best steakhouses in town. It's out on Southeast Stark Street, not too far from here."

"Driver, take us to The Old Country Kitchen," Luke said with enthusiasm.

It seemed that the incident at Sylvia's house was forgotten for the time being.

CHAPTER 34

The police arrived at the door of Luke and Geraldine's suite at the Hilton Hotel at 9:00 A.M. on the day after Christmas. Both Luke and Geraldine were still in bed and had bad hangovers after their night out at the steakhouse.

Luke got out of bed and staggered to the door. He was surprised to see the police there.

"We are here for Geraldine Rogers Payne. She is to accompany us to the station for questioning," the officer told Luke.

Luke yelled into the bedroom, "Sweet girl, the police want to see you. Better get a robe on before you come out."

Geraldine stumbled out of the bedroom with a deep scowl on her face, yelling at Luke to quiet down; she had a headache.

"Geraldine Rogers Payne?" the policeman asked.

"What do you want so early in the morning?" Geraldine inquired rudely.

"Better get some clothes on, ma'am. You are to accompany us to the police station for questioning in the Darren Polk arson and murder case. Officer Patterson will go with you," the police officer told Geraldine.

Officer Linda Patterson stepped into the room and took Geraldine by the arm to lead her into her bedroom.

Luke stood in the center of the room with his mouth hanging open. He didn't know what was going on and had the feeling that it was time to end his relationship with Geraldine. Things were getting too complicated. With a no-contact order in place for her to stay away from her daughter, and now being hauled to the police station for investigation of an arson and murder, it was getting pretty intense. He didn't want to get involved with any murder investigation.

When Geraldine and the policewoman came out of the bedroom, she said to Luke, "This is all a misunderstanding. I will clear it all up and be home by lunchtime. We can have a pleasant afternoon together."

Geraldine kissed Luke and reluctantly left with the policewoman.

When Geraldine had left, Luke showered and dressed, packed his bags, and called the porter to come and get them. He buzzed the front desk to ask them to have his bill ready; he was checking out immediately.

When Luke got to the front desk, he gave the receptionist money to give to one of the maids. He wanted her to go in and pack all of Mrs. Rogers' belongings and bring them to the main desk to hold until she could pick them up.

Geraldine arrived at the Multnomah County Police Station, grumbling about the fact that she had not had a cup of coffee yet and why she was being taken to the station anyway. Geraldine was still partially drunk and was having a hard time comprehending what was going on.

She was placed in an interrogation room and was brought a cup of good, strong coffee. Geraldine was very grateful for the coffee. She needed it to try to calm her nerves and wake her up.

Geraldine couldn't understand what was going on or why she was sitting in this room at the police station. She hadn't done anything wrong. A tall man walked into the room along with a policewoman and another police detective.

"Hello, Mrs. Payne," the tall man said. "My name is Bill Bowen. I am an arson investigator for the Multnomah County Fire Department. This is Officer Jan Malcolm, and this is Raymond Larson, a detective with the Multnomah County Sheriff 's Office. We want to ask you some questions about Darren Polk."

"I don't know any Darren Polk," Geraldine said sarcastically. "Yes, you do, Mrs. Payne," Detective Larson said. "He was the man who was with you the night you tried to break into your daughter's house."

"I never tried to break into my daughter's house. Why would I have to break in? She would let me come in anytime. We are on the best of terms. I see her all of the time," Geraldine explained. She was starting to get very nervous and talking very fast. She wondered what that little pip-squeak was trying to do now.

"Mrs. Payne, Darren Polk has accused you of being the mastermind in the arson fire that destroyed a property in Gresham, Oregon, that Payne Construction was building. As a result of that fire, the security guard, George Chamberlin, was killed. That is considered manslaughter in the State of Oregon. Mr. Polk has accused you of being the mastermind behind the arson," Bill Bowen explained to Geraldine.

"What?" Geraldine screamed as she got up suddenly from her chair, tipping the chair backward. "What in the hell is he saying about me? I don't even know the man. I would never condone arson, much less murder. Get my daughter down here. She will get me out of this mess."

"I'm sorry, Mrs. Payne. Your daughter has refused to see you. Where were you on the night of September 1, 1980?" asked Bill Bowen.

"I was on a cruise in the Caribbean with my fiancé, Luke Gregson. Ask him; he will verify that I was with him," Geraldine said, starting to panic.

"Mrs. Payne, I called the Hilton Hotel just before I came in here, and the receptionist at the hotel informed me that Mr. Gregson has checked out. He is flying back to his home in Oklahoma according to the receptionist," Detective Larson told her.

"Get me a lawyer! I am not saying another word without one," Geraldine announced.

"Do you have an attorney, Mrs. Payne?" the detective asked.

"I had one earlier this year. There was some small disagreement with my daughter, and I need to retain counsel. Call him! I don't remember his name; you will have to look it up on the records," Geraldine said.

"Mrs. Payne, we cannot call your attorney for you. You will have to do that. If you cannot get an attorney, one will be appointed to you from the public defender's office," the policewoman said.

"I don't care. Just get me an attorney," Geraldine yelled.

As Geraldine was yelling at the police, Luke was on a plane back to Tulsa. Geraldine's personal belongings from the hotel room were safely stored in a back room at the reception desk, and Jason and Sylvia were enjoying a quiet afternoon at home. It was wet and rainy outside and not a day that they wanted to be out doing the after-Christmas shopping as, according to the news, everyone else was. The shops and malls were packed with people looking for after-Christmas bargains.

Jason and Sylvia were looking through the Sears catalog, planning the baby's nursery. A new technology was being developed now called ultrasound. It would allow a couple to know the gender of their child before it was born. Neither Jason nor Sylvia felt that the technology was developed enough for them to take the risk, so they opted to be surprised.

They had picked out the crib, bassinet, and a dresser. She used to have the old rocking chair that was in her dad's bedroom, but it was smashed during the vandalism of her home.

"Could we go to some antique stores and see if we can find a rocking chair? We could possibly have it refinished if necessary. I did a lot of curling up in my daddy's lap in that rocking chair. I would love to be able to do that with my baby," Sylvia mentioned.

"Do you want to go looking tomorrow?" Jason asked her.

"Sure. That would be fun. You know, I am getting more and more excited about this baby as time goes on. I still want to go to the childcare classes to learn how to take care of a baby, and I think we need to attend some childbirth classes a little later on," Sylvia was saying.

Just then the phone rang. They were both startled at the sound.

They were not expecting any phone calls on the day after Christmas.

"Hello, Gorman residence," Jason announced into the receiver. "Hello, Jason. Bill Bowen here. I wanted to let you know that we are detaining your mother-in-law for questioning in the arson and manslaughter case. She is here at the County jail and is extremely agitated, claiming she does not even know Darren Polk. We also found out that her friend, Luke Gregson, checked out of the hotel and is on his way back to Tulsa."

Bill continued, "She is saying that, quote, 'Her lovely daughter Sylvia will get her out of this,' unquote."

"Oh brother! This is all we need. Sylvia wants nothing to do with her. She does not want to see her at all," Jason expounded. "Does she have an attorney?"

"She couldn't remember the name of the one she had before. She said she had a 'small disagreement' with her daughter and had an attorney then. Do you remember who it was?" Bill asked.

"It was James Murray. She can try to get ahold of him, but I doubt if he will take the case. She did not get along with him at all and never would take his advice. He was very glad when he no longer had to represent her," Jason told Bill. "Thanks for the information. Good luck with her. She is a real handful."

"Your mother has been detained by Bill and Detective Ray Larson for questioning in the fire and George's death. That was Bill on the phone to let us know what was going on. She is apparently claiming that she does not even know a Darren Polk and that Luke Gregson is her fiancé," Jason said to Sylvia.

"You know, I don't care at this point. I want to concentrate on our baby and decorating the nursery. I want to go out today and find a rocking chair and whatever else we can find for the baby's room. Reality will raise its ugly head on the 5th when we have to be in court for the trial. I will have to see my mother then, but I am not going to worry about that now," Sylvia announced.

"Good for you, sweetheart!" Jason said as he hugged her. "Let's get ready and go to the antique stores."

CHAPTER 35

January 5, 1971, Jason and Sylvia Gorman were sitting in the Multnomah County courtroom for the trial of Darren Polk for the arson of the office building in Gresham and the death of George Chamberlin. He was charged with arson and manslaughter. Geraldine Rogers Payne was also in the courtroom, sitting between two Multnomah County policemen. She was dressed in a very frumpy-looking dress that someone would have worn in the 1950s as a house dress. She had a very flowery hat on her head, and her hair was not groomed in its usual meticulous way. Something was definitely wrong with her.

Sylvia leaned over to Jason and said very quietly, "She looks strange. I have never seen her look so unkempt."

"Let's watch and see how she reacts to the testimony," Jason said. "I think she is scheduled to take the witness stand today."

The trial started with the prosecutor calling Bill Bowen to the stand. He testified to the fact that the fire was caused by an arsonist using gasoline to start the fire. He also testified that the body of George Chamberlin was found in the building, trapped under some fallen beams.

The coroner testified that George Chamberlin was killed by smoke inhalation. He was not badly burned and could have survived his injuries if the beams had not fallen on him and trapped him in the building.

Jason was then put on the witness stand to testify about Payne Construction having the contract to build the building and the condition of the construction site when he arrived there right after the fire. "George Chamberlin was a very neat and tidy man. His paperwork was always done correctly, and his reports were very accurate. When I viewed the construction shack where his desk was, it was a mess. Papers were tossed all over the office, and chairs and tables were upended. George would never have left the office in that condition."

Sylvia was called to the stand after Jason. As she was walking up to the witness stand, Geraldine hollered out to her, "Hi there, Sylvia. How you doing'?"

Sylvia ignored her as she sat down in the witness chair. Geraldine hollered out, "That's my daughter. Isn't she pretty?

I taught her all she knows about the construction business. She's real smart. Gets it from me!" Geraldine ranted on.

"Order in the court!" the judge yelled as he pounded his gavel on the desk. "Officers, please keep that lady quiet."

Sylvia testified to the financial loss caused by the fire. It was a financial loss not only to Payne Construction but to the City of Gresham.

After Sylvia testified, the judge called a 15-minute recess. When court convened again, Geraldine was called to the stand. She sauntered up to the witness chair, sat down, and pulled her dress up over her knees. "I'm ready for your questions now," she announced.

"Mrs. Payne, where were you on the night of September 1, 1970?" the prosecutor asked.

"First of all, call me Geraldine. I respond better to that than Mrs. Payne. I was on a cruise ship in the Caribbean with my fiancé, Luke Gregson. We were having such a good time. Have you ever been on a cruise? You should go on one. They are really fun," Geraldine said eagerly.

"Mrs. Payne, do you know the gentleman sitting at the defense table?" the prosecutor asked her.

"I don't think I have had the pleasure, but I would like to meet him. He's cute!" Geraldine commented.

"Mrs. Payne, on May 12, 1970, you were on trial for trying to break into your daughter's home and slandering her and her business in the newspapers. Is that true?"

"I don't remember that!" Geraldine said with wide eyes. "I don't think I was ever on trial for anything. I really would like to see my fiancé, Luke Gregson. Do you think you could ask him to come here and pick me up?"

"Your Honor, I think that this witness is incapable of testifying at this time. Maybe she should be seen by medical personnel," the prosecutor suggested.

"You are excused, Mrs. Payne," the judge said.

"Thank you," Geraldine answered. "Will you call Luke for me?

I need him to come and pick me up."

The two police officers escorted Geraldine out of the courtroom and took her to a holding cell until they could get some medical assistance for her.

Darren Polk was the next witness to testify. He chose to testify, hoping that it would help in lowering the length of his sentence.

"Mr. Polk, did you set the fire at the Gresham, Oregon construction site on September 1, 1970?" the prosecutor asked Darren.

"Yes, I did. Geraldine said it would be an easy way to put the screws to her daughter and cause her to lose the business. Geraldine wanted that business. She promised me a lot of money when she got control of it. I didn't expect the guard to go into the building. It was a really stupid thing for him to do. I didn't mean for anyone to die. It was Geraldine's offer of money that caused me to set the fire," Darren tried to explain.

"Mr. Polk, did you at one time try to break into Sylvia Payne's home at the behest of her mother?" the prosecutor asked.

"I did some time in jail for that," Darren answered. "Your Honor, I am finished with the prosecution's case." The judge called on the defense to present their case.

"Your Honor, the accused has chosen to change his plea to guilty and will accept the punishment given to him," Darren's attorney said.

"The defendant's change of plea is accepted by this court. I am issuing a bench warrant for the arrest of Geraldine Rogers Payne on the charge of conspiracy to commit arson and manslaughter," the judge said. "Bailiff, please see that Mrs. Payne is detained. Court dismissed," the judge said as he pounded his gavel.

Sylvia sat in the courtroom, stunned at what she had seen and heard. Her mother was either putting on a show for the judge or she had really gone off the deep end. She wasn't sure, but she knew she did not want to have any contact with her now. The safety of her husband and baby were what she cared about now. She wanted to get back to work and run her business the best way she could. She wanted to have her baby in June and maybe someday have some more babies. And most of all, she wanted to be free to come and go as she pleased and not worry about whether the guards were on duty or whether the alarms were turned on.

www.ingramcontent.com/pod-product-compliance
Lightning Source LLC
Chambersburg PA
CBHW031054310726
48969CB00007B/2264